On A Slant

A Collection of Stories

Celia H. Miles

Copyright © 2003 by Celia H. Miles

ISBN 0-7414-1545-3

Published by:

PUBLISHING.COM

519 West Lancaster Avenue
Haverford, PA 19041-1413
Info@buybooksontheweb.com
www.buybooksontheweb.com
Toll-free (877) BUY BOOK
Local Phone (610) 520-2500
Fax (610) 519-0261

Printed in the United States of America

Printed on Recycled Paper

Published June 2003

Table of Contents

These stories are dedicated
to my women friends—one and all.

Alabaster's Mill

"To think I gave up palm trees for this godforsaken place."

Shay replaced the sheet of paper as carefully as she had so carelessly picked it up and glanced at it. That's what I get, she thought, for reading somebody else's mail. Even if it wasn't mailed yet, just a scribbled half-page. Even if it was written by my husband.

She knew then Jack would be leaving.

Shay turned to the window and rubbed its wetness away. The condensed air on the inside gave her a sense of enclosure and safety even when the room temperature read less than fifty. The stream glistened with ice at its edges but ran swiftly in the center. Shay welcomed the December cold snap after a lingering and lovely fall. Finally the season had asserted itself in the North Carolina mountains and for three days the thermometer had not risen to the high thirties. She leaned forward to look more closely at the waters of the Little Broad River. Her breath misted again the window. She went down the stairs to the warmth of the kitchen. Jack would not be up for another hour or two.

Into strong black tea, Shay tossed in two heaping spoons of brown sugar. She sat at the oak table, warming her hands against the cup. Wondering what the pre-Christmas chill would bring to her and Jack. "Oh Shay," he might say in a voice neither quite resigned nor quite happy, "I'm okay. We can make it here." She doubted it.

The letter was addressed to his mother. Jack wrote to her every week. When they met, Shay had admired Jack's

1

concern for his sixty-five year old mother. In his mid-thirties still living at home, Jack truly liked his mother and she allowed herself to be liked, to be driven about the city, to be taken out to eat at Mario's on special occasions or for pizza on Wednesday nights before her bingo game. Jack told her when he'd be home or when he was sleeping over somewhere. Mrs. Ormand surprised her soon-to-be daughter in law by declaring, "I wish you all the best."

All the best had assumed that Jack would keep his position at the software company and that Shay would be content in the sunny jungle of Miami. And so it was--for three years. Shay measured those years by the gradual wisping away of Mrs. Ormand's physical abilities. First, she endured gall bladder surgery, then she fell. She used a walker mostly, a cane occasionally. Jack attended her with obvious devotion.

Shay was short for Shadow, a name her hippy-before-hippies-were-cool mother had stuck her with. Actually, it was the only thing her mother had ever given her that she liked. Her mother had named her Shadow rather than Sunshine when in the last days of pregnancy her lover deserted her in a lonely western town. Shay had not known her mother, however, because six months after Shadow's birth, Alice Macon, now calling herself "Gaia," left Shay in a boot box outside the Methodist parsonage. Seven years later, the minister's wife told Shay of her mother and the name shift and that Alice Macon had been the victim of the flu and malnourishment. She didn't say that drugs had contributed to her mother's death, but the first grader sensed that the death hadn't been from "approved" causes. Shay grew up in a series of homes in and around Blowing, Montana, being an easy child to care for and love. In her first foster home when the four-year son lisped only the initial syllable, Shadow became Shay.

At eighteen, after her high school graduation, Shay said goodbye to all the folks who had cared for her--for love or money or both--said goodbye to Montana forever, and got on the bus with two suitcases and a ticket to Chicago. Some

2

years later, the memory of a beach postcard she'd seen when she was thirteen surfaced. And since she wanted to go somewhere, she settled easily on Florida.

A truck shifted gears and crawled up the hill; Shay waited until silence followed before setting her cup on the table. The direct heat from the kitchen stove kept her toes hot; her ears and the tip of her nose, though, were cold. But she had grown used to one part of her body being toasty while another was icy. She liked it. She liked living in this mill on the banks of the Little Broad, liked hearing the thump-thud of the wheel turning, liked the constancy of the river sounds. She thought of the events that had brought her here. Fate surely--for here she was happy.

"Fucking weird!" Jack had studied the deed as if it were a rare black pearl. "I don't believe it!" He'd held it up to the Miami sunset and read it again.

Shay couldn't believe it either. But there it was: delivered by priority mail as promised. Three weeks earlier she had been drinking alone at a bar not far from her office. Correction: not far from her previous office. She'd been assistant to the news director at the local television station, secure in her position, not particularly ambitious. No threat to any of the bright young women and handsome young men who arrived at WSIM to start their upward climb in the profession. She and Jack had been married long enough for the excitement to become routine spiced occasionally with love and good times. Then the blow. Her job was being terminated; as the station downsized, various people could pick up various aspects of her responsibilities. Good references, insurance for a couple of months, a severance check the following Friday.

Well, there were other jobs and she would find one. She had several positions before WSIM: waitress, student, receptionist at the community college, copywriter for local tourist newspapers, secretary at the station. So she wasn't exactly crying in her beer as she contemplated her situation. She'd hardly noticed the wizened white-haired man talking to the bartender. Then he shambled over to the end of the bar

3

and threw a few darts with careless ease at the board. She saw he was very good.

"Care to give it a try?"

Cass at the bar raised his voice. "Hey, Shay, he's talking to you."

During her first waitressing job, Shay had whiled away hours throwing darts, and her friends envied her smooth and accurate delivery. She looked again at the old man, pale in the darkness, pale even in the glow of pink neon. Just a lonely old geezer was her estimate. What the hell. She wasn't doing anything except feeling put upon by the male world at large and Jack in particular. He'd chosen not to accompany her, opting instead for a visit to his mother.

"Want to take me on, little lady?" The old man flipped a dart up into the air and caught it deftly in his left hand. The bartender smirked, bored with only the two customers in the pre-pre dinner hour.

The "little lady" provoked Shay to stretch luxuriously and yawn, demonstrating disdain and some contempt. "Show me what you can do," she told him. She didn't want him to think she'd noticed just how good he was.

"I'm Alabaster Sutton," the man said, looking at her. At the same time, the dart made a resounding thunk just slightly off center. "Call me Al, if you want."

Shay admired the throw enough to get up from the booth and shake his hand. His hand was dry, boney, the fingernails clean and cut short. He took care of his hands. No rings. No watch on his thin wrist. "Okay, Al. You're on."

"No money in it?" asked the bartender.

"A couple of rounds warm up," Shay countered, "and then we'll see."

Neither of them played up to their potential in the first rounds; Shay deliberately didn't and she was fairly sure Alabaster was holding back. An hour later after each had won and lost and Cass kept score, serving the few other patrons quickly so he could watch the exchange, Al had pulled ahead by fifteen dollars. Shay said, "Let me buy you a beer and get out of here. Jack will be wondering where I am." As they nursed their final drinks, the old man didn't ask a lot of questions, didn't ask any, in fact, but she found herself telling him about Jack and about her job. His washed-out eyes reminded her of the early morning light blue haze on the bay, not intense but drawing her in. She left almost reluctantly.

"How about a rematch day after tomorrow?" Al said.

"Great. I'll be here to win my money back."

His eyes lit up as if the sun were rising behind them. "Same time, then."

For two weeks Shay met Alabaster at the pub; for two weeks they competed fiercely. Then she sensed a slackening off in her opponent's moves. Not that he obviously let her win; that she would have not allowed. And she couldn't be sure. They were evenly matched. Are we just playing games, she wondered, as she picked up the $37 from the bar, games within games?

One night after the old man left she asked Cass about him. "He always comes and goes in a cab," he told her. "Don't know where exactly."

"Well, is he serious about playing forever, you think?" Shay had to get a job soon and the only ones she'd been offered were evenings and part-time.

"Seems like it." Cass returned to his customers. "But he's a strange old bird."

"Not local," Shay said. "He's pale as a ghost."

The next day Alabaster appeared later than usual and paler. "You okay?" Shay asked.

"As well as I'm going to get," Al said. A missing button on his shirt cuff allowed the sleeve to ride up, revealing his wrist. As his arm rested on the edge of the bar, she noticed an indentation, the hair slightly moist and matted as if a watch had been removed. Al always wore long sleeved shirts, either light green checks or stark white. His fingers trembled a little as he lifted his beer. Cass now routinely waved aside payment. As their bouts had

5

continued, customers started dropping in to watch the games. They were good for business.

In an hour or so, Al owed Shay almost a hundred dollars; he had insisted on upping the bet every time. Finally she said, "That's it for me, Al." She touched his shoulder lightly. "I don't want to take all your money!"

"Let's sit over there for a few minutes," he said. In the booth he told her he didn't have any money to pay up, just enough for a cab "back," but he put his proposition to her. A final game: "I win-- double my money. You win you get all I've got left in the world." He wouldn't say what that was, but his watery eyes brightened as she tried to cajole him into revealing what she was playing for. Al simply said, "It's all I ever prized--and didn't know it till too late." He stood up. "Don't let that happen to you."

Their last game brought the customers crowding close to watch. Point for point, they threw. Shay drew ahead and Al threw crazy wide. "Hey!" she protested.

Al shrugged and dragged himself onto a stool. He put out his hand. "Thanks for the games, young lady. Look for your prize in the mail in a couple of days." He turned to Cass, "Call me a cab, will you? I'm late as it is."

Shay realized how tired he was. She hugged him lightly, for fear of crushing his frail body. "You're the best," she said. The crowd applauded as he made his way to the door.

Thus she became the owner of Alabaster Sutton's Mill in Matlowe County, on the banks of The Little Broad River. Shay had never been to the western part of North Carolina and she wasn't sure what to expect. Jack told her, "You'll be back in Miami in two months."

Shay wanted to see her mill alone. She left the Asheville law office at six o'clock with assurances she would be near Wren before dark. The directions were clear. The mill stood on the side of state highway 203, two miles from the crossroads of Wren and five miles from the county seat of Matlowe. As she rounded the curve just before the mill, her coffee slopped over. She felt tilted to the right. The highway seemed to be slipping into the river, at least temporarily. The right hand side of the highway was an inch or so lower for a good fifty feet.

The mill stood tall, very close to the pavement with maybe eight feet separating the asphalt from its front wall. She pulled into a weedy parking area which itself was separated from the stream by an iron single pipe running between cement blocks and some unidentifiable low bushes and what she later could recognize as Queen Anne's Lace. The water beyond her car was still, hardly moving, caught near the bank; farther out the river flowed gently toward the dilapidated dam which was only three quarters there. When the river's waters reached the barrier they simply swirled toward the openings and continued with a muted rushing sound.

Shay's eyes followed the water, her ears soaking in the muffled movement for two or three minutes before she turned to the mill itself. Large, a functional rectangle set on its end, it couldn't be called lovely. It probably didn't merit a single picture postcard in the racks of the area's stores. It was covered with a grayish-black speckled tar paper, with some patches missing. The roof, of tin, painted a dull red, looked in good shape which meant the interior was dry.

The metal wheel hugged the side of the building. Its buckets held a collection of debris, sticks, tattered paper, a crumpled beer can, a sprinkling of green showing through. The grass or weeds made Shay smile; things would grow, given a smidgen of soil and a drop of rainwater. She squared her shoulders and went in search of a door to match the key the lawyer had given her. "This is the only key I've got," he said. "It's bound to open one of the doors. Just keep trying." Now she saw one door facing the highway and one at the side where she had stood--connected to nothing; on the lower level on the other side of the building was another. The ground was muddy, squishy beneath her shoes, and she wondered what she'd do if the key didn't fit this lock. The door came open with a slight push and Shay was inside her mill.

A whiteness astonished Shay--the beams, the wheels, the cogs, barrels, all were covered with a soft filmy white powder. Two streaks of sunlight illuminated the otherwise dusky dark room. Shay stood, enchanted. She walked slowly, bumping her head and her elbows occasionally in the snowy gloom, running her fingers over the powdery residue of the milling process. Cobwebs were faintly white in the corners. The machinery seemed to be waiting, waiting to be set once again in motion. Shay wandered into the upstairs portion of the building, going from room to room, noting the various ropes, pulleys, ingenious devices which she could not name, noting the wide solid counter space, the limp cloth bags, the farming implements that had apparently been stored there. On the third floor, she sat down on a wooden chest and looked around her. *I can live here. I will live here.* She may have said the words aloud; certainly they resounded in her head in the silence of the tall deserted building.

In the months that followed, Shay detached herself from Florida completely. The sands, the streets, the few friends--all retreated as if they were an alien world. She moved sleeping bag and books, lanterns and kitchen utensils to her new home.

Shay haunted the little town closest to the mill. She sat in the BlueBird Cafe and talked to whoever came in. Gradually she met a man who in his teens had worked at the mill and who now did some carpentry work, some masonry work, some electrical work, who agreed to take a look at the mill. Within a few weeks, the electricity was restored, the plumbing worked, and corners were cobweb-free. Shay had worked miracles, mostly with a heavy-duty broom and vacuum cleaner. Her back hurt, her shoulder blades hurt, her calves ached, but the migraines she'd occasionally dealt with had not once recurred.

She sometimes sat and listened to the muffled swirl of the river as it flowed toward the French Broad and then the Gulf of Mexico. Her money had run out and she skimped even on food in order to pay the basic utilities. As summer reached its zenith, visitors stopped by now and then.

"Hey, I saw you at the BlueBird last week. Remember we talked about my great uncle who remembered old man..." a visitor would announce. Then, "I brought you some sweet corn and a mess of green beans. You know how to cook green beans?"

After a few such visits, Shay wondered if she looked hungry. She always invited the people in and showed them around; they supplied her with fresh vegetables, molasses ("last year's workings"), eggs, and honey. She became a vegetarian. And at the BlueBird, BB no longer handed her a menu. "Got good meatloaf today, Shay, but I can fix you a vegetable plate. Hot cornbread right out of the oven."

In mid-December, Jack arrived with the rental moving truck, cursing the mountains' curves. Both of them found part-time work, work that paid enough to barely cover their living expenses. Jack drove into Asheville to fill in at the public radio station. The best part of his job, he said, was access to the latest CDs and tapes. Shay waited tables on busy weekends and occasional evenings at an old inn some miles away. Then she agreed to work at the weekly county newspaper while the owner's wife took maternity leave. There she had time to research the old mills of the area and the milling operation. In between jobs she prowled around her mill, becoming as familiar with its every corner and piece of machinery as if she were its mother and it a child needing attention.

Jack turned aside from her one night. "You smell of cornmeal," he muttered. Shay had soaked her tired body in bubble bath and had scrubbed away the waitress smells. She knew what he said wasn't true. But the smell of cornmeal permeated the mill, sometimes more strongly than others. That rejection was the beginning of Jack's diminishing interest--in her, in the mill, in his job. For weeks, Shay ignored the February iciness that mirrored the freezing along the edges of the Little Broad. The winter invigorated her. During the inn's season Shay spent more and more time at the mill. She allowed its latent power to cloak her in stillness that she knew could break into movement and activity when it was time.

When Shay found the letter, Jack had been less than a full year at the mill. He had begun to look harried, his eyes slanted sideways when she tried to talk to him, he lost weight and looked unhealthy. The rain was too wet for him, the drought too dry, the winter too cold, and the autumn "dusty and depressing." She grew accustomed to Jack's absence even as he sat across the table from her or lay listless beside her.

When she held out the unmailed letter, he stuck it in the fire and announced that he was returning to Florida.

"Mother needs me. You don't. I can't live here," he said. "You keep the furniture."

Shay hugged him briefly, noting the boniness of his shoulder blades. "You get the divorce, will you? It'll be easier there."

He nodded, already moving toward the racks and stacks of CD's and tapes.

How easy, Shay thought, to end a marriage. She liked her husband then. They parted like distant cousins whom family ties had bound briefly together but who found nothing else in common.

Life was simpler without Jack, without having to consider when he'd be home, what mood he'd be in, what foods he would eat, what people in Wren he might chat with or might ignore on the streets. In early March she paused outside the town library. A child had left a kite on the grass and weighed it down with a backpack of books; another kite floated freely, lightly dipping and swooping though bound by a string to a youngster's hand. Now I'm like that kite, she thought, free to soar or to fall, always attached to something I love. Shay laughed aloud.

"Something funny?" Mr. Stanton, from the bank, asked as he headed toward the BlueBird.

"I'm just thinking in mixed metaphors," she said. He shook his head as if he agreed.

So Shay subsisted. She scratched out a tiny garden between the highway and the river, listening to the old-timers' advice about planting when the signs were just right for her four hills of cabbage and for her row of pole beans. She grew wiry, lean; she grew graceful from learning to move efficiently in and out of tight places. She determined to re-open the mill and to operate it--at a loss or not. The bank couldn't see its way clear to make a loan, but Mr. Stanton himself and the BlueBird owner made personal loans to her with only her handwritten IOU.

"What's a few thousand?" BB shrugged, "If you don't get it, I'll have to shell out for my grandkids' college."

"Shell out!" Mr. Stanton quipped. "Put your nose to the grindstone, Shay, and pay me whenever...before the nursing home gets me, anyway." Shy, staid Mr. Stanton exhibited a wittiness as he and Shay drank coffee and shared the morning paper that he didn't demonstrate in his Vice President's office at the bank.

While she studied books and talked and even attended a conference on old mills, Shay worked eighteen hours a day when possible, saving money, and making plans. She might have become totally obsessed with her mill if not for her "paying" jobs. She liked the people around her, smiled easily, paid no attention to things like unpainted fingernails, uncouth hair cuts, and unglossed lips. When, usually wearily, she returned to the mill, she became both invigorated and serene. She cleaned, polished, scraped at rust, paint; she pored over catalogs, brochures, old books which enlarged her understanding of mill equipment; sometimes she sat with her hot tea and listened to the river. She hoped she could use the present wheel but she wasn't sure. She needed to know more.

Mr. Stanton tried to fix her up with his middle boy who was finalizing a divorce; two dates nixed that. BB didn't push, but he said, "When you're ready, I can name a couple of guys maybe worth your time." She slept, after a fine dinner at the Marketplace and fine liquors later, with a fast-talking sales rep staying at the inn. They parted mutually satisfied, and Shay told herself: "I can't start this."

Tomblin Field walked into the mill on a cloudy

afternoon. He had a backpack, sturdy boots, a two-days' beard, and no inclination to talk.

"I can help with that," he told her. Shay stopped pushing the heavy wooden chest and wiped the perspiration from her forehead. She stood aside while he slipped the backpack to the floor and then together they slid the chest to the place she'd cleared for it.

"What else?" He looked around.

Shay thought she might as well take advantage of this free help. She went to get supplies while he looked around, and he followed her to the wheel. She had not wanted to risk cleaning it alone and she resisted the idea of allowing just anybody to share the task. He was perfect; he'd be moving on.

Except he didn't move on. She directed him with a minimum of words as they sweated at the wheel; he didn't contradict her or attempt to dominate the job. When they'd finished as much as daylight would permit, Shay offered lentil soup and homemade bread and a chance to wash up. Only when they were seated at the table, a kerosene lamp between them, did it occur to Shay to introduce herself.

"I'm Tomblin Field," he responded, breaking the crusty bread delicately.

"Where are you headed?" Shay asked. "Where are you staying?"

The man looked at her. His brown eyes caught her own green ones for a long moment. His hands rested on the table edge as if they'd been there days and weeks.

"Okay," Shay said.

Tomblin Field stayed at the mill for three months, sharing Shay's bed from the first hour after their shared meal. She had not been sure what would happen. After a quick clean up in the kitchen she announced, "I'm going to bed," and gestured towards the stairs.

"Okay." The slight smile that had played around his lips at the dinner table turned full; he had perfect teeth.

BB at the BlueBird teased Shay later that a smile never left her eyes during the months Tomblin was at the mill. "But he sure don't talk much," BB said.

"Doesn't need to," Shay grinned. BB gave her a thumbs up and resumed scrubbing the counter top.

With Jack Shay had tried to communicate her feelings about the mill, tried to elicit his feelings about their life together, but with Tomblin she did not ask another question about his life. He was here; he was now. She was happy. When he brought his backpack downstairs three months later, she wasn't surprised. Outside their bed, Tomblin had never kissed her; he didn't kiss her as he hoisted his pack and walked to the highway. In the doorway Shay asked, "Can I drive you to Asheville?"

"Thanks for it all. No." He tilted slightly toward the river as he walked on the highway. She wandered through the mill, around the mill, sat and watched the wheel turn, balanced, clean, steady. He had made it possible. They had managed to grind enough meal so that she knew she could handle the job. They held a semi-open house, making no public announcements, but dozens of people stopped by to marvel at what Shay and her stranger had accomplished. She gave meal to her friends and promised to charge them for the next batch. In all her life she had never been as happy as when that first white meal shifted into sight--except, perhaps, as the night Tomblin had appeared, naked and white in the moonlight, at her bed.

It was a hard year for Shay. Physically hard, economically hard. She ground very little meal, but she developed her marketing plan, got some notice in the Asheville paper, prepared her sign for the tourist season: Alabaster Mill. Most local people simply called it the mill but she intended to honor the memory of Alabaster who had died far away from his property and who had cheated at darts to assure that she would have it.

When Tomblin reappeared--again just as she needed him, frustrated that the high school football player had not shown up to work as promised--Shay did not pretend surprise. She did not have to pretend pleasure. He looked exactly the same.

"New boots?" she said.

"The old one gave up their soles in Tullahoma." He heaved his backpack to a nearby chair. They grinned at each other.

"Coffee first?"

"I could use some." Tomblin went to the kitchen and took down mugs while Shay washed her oily hands.

"There's a lot to do before the season really gets going," Shay said. "I want to open up to the public next Saturday."

He nodded, and they settled into their routine.

After Alabaster Mill's second season, Shay told Mr. Stanton and BB, "I can pay my bills now and soon start paying you two back." She continued her two jobs because something was always breaking down or needing attention. Tomblin tended the mill. He couldn't cook but he could stir whatever she left simmering on the stove, and the inn insisted on sending leftovers home after her shift. They ate well. They played double solitaire some evenings, but most of the time they went to bed early and rose early. Shay wondered whether to tell Tomblin that she'd missed him, that his side of the bed had not been slept in since he left. She didn't.

After the fourth season Shay found that she was pregnant. He was gone; she was thirty-six. Different doctors had told her that she needn't take the pill; pregnancy was not an option. She went to a doctor in Asheville with all the signs, which she did not recognize.

When Tomblin stepped into the mill some nine months later, he saw the tiny cradle on the counter top, saw the tiny girl with green eyes before he saw Shay. A flicker of uncertainty shadowed his eyes as he looked around, perhaps for evidence of the presence of a man. He saw none. Lowering his backpack almost reverently, he moved to pick up the baby. Shay had not been sure how she would respond if Tomblin returned, whether she would want to or could share the child. She helped him slip his large hand under the delicate bundle, making sure his other hand supported the

14

tiny head with its brown hair.

"I--I have to sit down," Tomblin said. He didn't bother to find a chair, simply slid to the floor in front of the counter. He held the baby carefully and looked at Shay.

"Being a father makes you swimmy-headed, does it?" she said. Old Mrs. Burton down the road often used those words to describe her condition. They fit the expression on Tomblin's face.

"That it does," he said. And again they resumed their life together. Being a mother might have accounted for Shay's increased curiosity about Tomblin. She wondered if he had children somewhere; he didn't seem squeamish about changing diapers or annoyed about being awakened by Allie's early morning cries. He watched Allie nursing as if he intended to write a book. Shay wondered, but she had determined not to question, not to ask any more of Tomblin than in the past seasons. He volunteered nothing, worked hard, assumed all the husbandly and fatherly duties and pleasures--and smiled broadly as people in the BlueBird came by their booth to admire their beautiful baby. People had stopped asking Shay about him, not realizing that she knew nothing except his name and the typical time of his reappearance each year.

Alabaster's Mill and Allie flourished under Shay's love and attention. She became the topic of an article on women in milling and she was invited to attend SPOOM's meetings, at first as a curiosity and then as an expert. Allie went with her in a papoose sack and then holding on to her hand. Tomblin saw Allie for her first five years and then he failed to appear. Allie did not call him daddy, and she asked, "When's Tom coming home, Mama?"

Shay only shook her head. "Maybe not this year, Allie."

Night after night, Shay sat outside, looking at the wheel, listening to its clunky rhythm. She often kept the wheel running even when its power was not used because she liked the sound it made. Some two and a half weeks after the time Tomblin would have normally appeared, she stood

15

at the table, making a pot of tea before going out of doors. Something wasn't right. She checked the stove, she looked in on Allie. She poured her tea, a sickness passing over her, making her feel faint. Something was missing. She concentrated. It was the absence of the clunky turning of the wheel. The silence overwhelmed her and she sat down. Absolute silence from the wheel; only the muffled sound of the river. She knew she had to go check on the wheel; in its predictability she found comfort. Yet for several minutes she sat unmoving. Her heart thudded violently as the clunk of the wheel resumed. The buckets swished their offerings. She would not see Tomblin again. That she knew. In some deeper part of herself, deep as the repaired dam, she knew he was dead--and she knew when his heart had stopped.

"What do you think, BB?" Mr. Stanton asked his friend two years later. "Our loans, with interest, are paid in full from his estate. There's enough for a little backlog for Shay since she's been paying us a little all along. It's taken this long for his will to be probated and all the legalities to be taken care of. The question is: how do I tell her?"

"She knows." BB scrubbed the sink. "She has known."

The Buttons

Holly twisted the thread connecting the purple button on her blazer cuff and kept twisting it, concentrating on its double thickness, determined to conquer, to separate the button from its indented space. She knew that the woman sitting opposite had been watching for some time, maybe willing the button to resist. As the thread broke, Holly had the urge to push the purple button up her own nose, to astonish the woman, to cause some small degree of consternation in the room. She stared at the button, balancing it on an upturned forefinger, tempted to bring it to her nostril.

"Mrs. Noland, please." The nurse waited for Holly to precede her into Dr. Wesson's office. Holly looked at the button and then pushed it into the fake soil of the fake plant on the table beside the green vinyl sofa. Holly winked at the woman whose mouth was now a little o and followed the nurse.

"No luck this time, Mrs. Noland." The doctor snapped something shut with a click. "Don't give up hope yet." He washed his hands. "I'm referring you to a colleague in Baltimore. Dr. Dannois has a reputation for cracking tough cases." He handed a slip of paper to the nurse. "The office will set up the appointment." One more woman trying to get pregnant. In this case, one more defeat for him.

Dr. Dannois' office was small, decorated in pastels: pink and blue and yellow. The flowers were real, the sofa a soft floral fabric. Holly waited with one other patient, a girl, surely too young to be here. Holly's suit had brass buttons imprinted with lions. She started working on the lowest button on the jacket, the most accessible. She waited two hours in Dr. Dannois' office and the button perversely took forever. She twisted methodically minute after minute until the girl could not ignore the activity but could not acknowledge it either. She inspected the prints of hovering sea gulls, leaving Holly to concentrate furiously. The thread broke after a final brutal twist and the button rolled down Holly's thigh and under the nearby table. Holly looked with satisfaction at its space and got down on her knees to seek the button. She wiped wisps of dust lint from it as if brushing straw from a boy's curls. Approaching the plant, she poked her finger into the soft dirt, shoving the button close to the roots of the tulip.

The nurse announced: "Mrs. Noland, this way please." The girl turned and Holly lifted her eyebrows elaborately, as if they'd shared a joke.

"I want you to see Dr. Meizel, as soon as he can set up an appointment." Dr. Dannois semi-slumped into a chair opposite Holly. "He's the best. I think you'll like him." Holly breathed deeply and stood. When she extended her hand, Dr. Dannois almost missed the gesture, turning as she was to make a final notation on the chart. "Ah, yes," she murmured. "And let me know, will you?"

In the waiting room, Holly worried first one fine white button, then another from the double buttoned cuff of her white blouse. As she twisted and pulled, she noticed the tiny freckles adorning the top of her hand but she did not allow them to distract her. Her intense concentration drew attention. One woman stopped reading *Parents* and simply stared, her lips slightly pursed. Another slopped a splash of coffee at the urn. Holly spent more than twenty minutes on the first button, seventeen on the next. The *Parents* reader clocked the second and breathed audibly when the button lay in Holly's hand, cupped with the other one. When the nurse appeared, Holly stood straight and smiled. She took the buttons over to the large Ficus tree in the corner and while the nurse held the door open, Holly carefully planted the buttons fairly close to each other. Brushing her soiled hands on her blue linen skirt, she wrinkled her nose and went into Dr. Meizel's office.

"What's this thing?" Dr. Wesson's receptionist, dusting the office plants, thought she saw a purple blossom among what she knew were fake flowers.

"What in the world?" Dr. Dannois' nurse examined the strangely golden, brassy looking tulip bloom.

"Strange," Dr. Meizel's patient said. Two little white flowers seemed out of place under the Ficus tree.

And miles away, Holly slept with her newborns cradled close.

Woman of the Stones

The fan droned and droned, a continuous sound that entered her very pores, that seeped, then drove into her being, that drowned out all else, prevented thought, and yet she was thinking oh my god, my god, my god in a circular motion, going nowhere, doing nothing, nothing, nothing.

In the next room the refrigerator droned and hummed, a giant mechanical gnat at the edge of her consciousness. A lawnmower suddenly whirred and rattled outside. In the hot room, surrounded by her books, Handra stared first at the ceiling and then twisted to watch the fan, willing it to perform its duties silently or simply to stop its movement. Her senses felt benumbed, dulled by the repetitiveness of sound.

Handra pushed *The Awakening* aside and reached for the British travel magazine close at hand, anything to keep at bay the clatter bombarding her eyebrows, her blue veined knees, her skull, her eyeballs. The tiny advertisement read: cottage in remote Orkneys for sale. $17,000 firm.

The Orkneys. She'd been there once with Clive. Remote, yes. A stop at John o' Groats and then a ferry from Scrabster, tossing waves. A two-night stay, a day-long tour. Grayness and greenness. Stone circles, standing megaliths, a burial mound. A village dating from some 5000 years ago uncovered by a storm in the 1800s: foundations grown over by lush grass, the sea lapping coldly close by. Handra closed her eyes, willing the droning of the fan to become the lapping of waves. It did: she saw a gray cottage set back on the moors within sound of the sea but safe from stormy onslaughts; she saw few trees, grass nibbled at by sheep and spotted cows, no lawnmowers; no heat waves, no fans; no air conditioners. She saw quietness. She looked at the ad and its e-mail address. She concentrated again and saw the interior of the cottage: a fridge, yes; an electric typewriter, yes; she couldn't quite see her computer in the cottage--not yet-- the stillness of dark early nights, heard the grumble of an occasional automobile over the moor, muted and perhaps comforting.

Within three weeks, Handra had arranged a leave of absence, easily enough. The head librarian had been almost too agreeable. Once she was out of his office, he smirked, "She needs something, that woman." Miss Hopewell muttered under her breath, "A man. Sex," not sure old Mr. Monroe would appreciate her appraisal of Handra Conard. Mr. Monroe was wondering if his young assistant's love life was as steamy as those novels she kept hidden in her desk behind her manicure implements would imply. So Handra left her job, met the realtor in Stromness, handed him a check eight days later, and stood looking at her property.

Alone. She had names of reliable workmen who could restore the cottage to livability: repair the roof, install modern plumbing, inspect and replace wiring, make the windows airtight. In Kirkwall and Stromness she could purchase simple furnishings. The agent had assured her that the large stove worked, as did the fireplace. Handra looked about her. Not a sound in sight. She had a two-months' leave, at the end of which she'd decide what to do. Her parents were dead; her one sister had some twenty years ago disappeared into a commune. Her friends, quite frankly, were mostly those Clive had brought to their relationship in his town. She'd been ultra thrifty with Clive's settlement and after a while, if she stayed, she could find work. Meanwhile, the realtor had lent her a sturdy bike with big tires. When she needed to go into town, he told her, she could peddle a mile or so to the nearest neighbor and ride with their two girls who had steady jobs.

The quietness created a sexual awareness in Handra, a stirring long absent, absent long before Clive's departure. She remembered the roaring of the room air conditioner in the coastal motel. It had been muted by the fury in his voice. She'd reported finally what the doctor had said. "I can't conceive. It's me. You don't have to worry about your virility."

She wished she'd known for months, months of sweaty angry sex. As he approached forty-five, Clive had become obsessed with having a child, exerting every effort to impregnate her. For a while, she'd enjoyed his renewed attentions. "After all," a friend said, "your biological clock is running. You're close to forty." When the sexual act became no more than a propagation act for Clive, she gritted her teeth, occasionally pinching her thigh to prevent a yawn. Clive accused her of psychologically blocking conception since his sperm count was consistently high. In those (as she now considered them) rutting months, sometimes she had wanted to blurt out, "It doesn't matter! Stop--" Once, a cliche had emerged in a giggling gasp, "Stop and smell the roses." Clive had not stopped but had remembered. "For God's sake, Handra, roses!" Around them the air stirred, sluggish as her body.

When the divorce date arrived, both signed the papers with Arctic coldness. Clive married again within six months and fathered a child within the year. Michelle sent a birth announcement with the quarterly payment.

Handra was pleased with the lichened cottage, delighted with the solitude, the quietness. She found she needed to talk very little. People made some initial efforts to engage this stranger who painted and hammered, who strove to learn weaving with deaf Mrs. Bowen. But she was not one for socializing.

Months passed, and she turned her leave of absence into official resignation without a thought. Handra became a familiar sight on the island: loose dark trousers, loosely woven sweaters, comfortably heavy boots, hair that grew and demanded a braid. Unerringly polite to all, she made some small talk with the shopkeepers, made no friends among the women but no enemies either. The widow Bowen taught Handra how to keep a fire going, how to recognize the call of birds, when to start seedlings in a sunny window, how to preserve apples. Who could be jealous of this not-so-young woman who gave her cosmetics and dresses to the neighbor's daughters and who spent solitary hours walking along the shore. When the workmen dealt with her, they told their wives and girlfriends she was friendly enough, offered strong tea, made fair scones, did not flirt with them. And it was all true.

When the September moon shone full on a Thursday night, Handra pulled on a sweater and wheeled her bike down the path to the smoother road. Half an hour later, leaving the bike in a hedge, she neared the ring of huge stones, the Stones of Stenness. She knew she was putting her feet down in a normal purposeful stride, but she felt as if she were floating slightly above the ground; light and easy. She circled the outside of the stones, then moved in the shadow of the largest stone. She circled from stone to stone, in and out of their shadows. Clouds darkened the moon and she shivered at the call she could not name. No one else was about; the night was as still and quiescent as the breath of an angel or a dead man. At some point, maybe she was simply tired, Handra lay down in the full stream of moonlight. Who can say what she thought, if she thought. Something in the moon released her. When she rose an hour or so later, Handra knew she was bound to Orkney; her body might return to Michigan but her spirit had acquired kinship with the earth and the moon and she felt forever at home.

Life might have gone on like that for years, forever, if not for Michael McClains. Observing that Handra did not like the noise of mechanical devices such as drills and saws, or even motors, the workers often cut their engines at the road and walked up the path to the cottage. So did Michael McClains. His mouth fell open when he looked through the open door; it was a cool October afternoon. Handra was stretched out on the sofa, naked from the waist down. One hand caressed her breast; the other-- Michael McClains had never realized that women did that. He stared, taking in the closed book on the table, the empty tea cup, the slow movements as she swayed under her hand. He had the presence of mind to bend down and remove his boots quietly. He also quickly undid his belt and stepped forward. Handra opened her eyes at the sound of the zipper and she kept them open as Michael McClains removed her hand and replaced it with his own. Not a word was spoken. She did not blush or protest; he did not ask or falter.

The interesting thing, Michael thought to himself-- and he must have told this thought to his brother Alex--was that Handra made not a sound during the entire-- "mating" was his word, being himself a shy man with women, even his wife.

"The silence," he said, trying to articulate carefully his experience on the sofa, "the silence was...it was beatific." His glare dared his brother to grin or to tease.

And so it happened that gradually Handra exchanged her "stranger" status for another. And so it happened, after Clive's checks ceased, that she could live with very little income. Occasionally Handra worked a few hours at the distillery, but office routines bored her. In time, the sale of her woolens provided sufficient ready cash. The cottage's roof was kept in repair, its plumbing in excellent shape, its tiny garden neat, its walls and paths well maintained. Fresh produce, fish, meat, and eggs arrived with or without a known deliverer. Quite often packets were simply left on the doorstep or on the kitchen table. Her doors were never locked. Of course, she lived simply: books, CDs, no jewelry, no cash, nothing of value. The cottage was rich in texture, however. Woolens, herbs, stones, bleached boards washed up from the sea --whatever appealed to Handra's senses as she walked or as she shopped; the cottage developed a patina over the years; the whitewashed walls mellowed, the smoke cast a soft grayness; the yellow curtains turned a muted beige. Darker reds and blues faded; dried mint and cow parsley filled vases, tins, pottery.

Handra had never been pretty; she did not become pretty. Men on the island could not explain her attractiveness for them; in some cases, their wives were slimmer, lovelier, livelier. In some cases, not. The plain fact is that the men who came to her in the afternoons, in the evenings, who strode to her door, who stumbled, who came in guilt or in sorrow, the men did not speak of Handra to each other. Their wives and girlfriends were not unaware that their men visited Handra. Yet how could they protest? She asked nothing of them; if she knew the size of this man's cock and that man's balls, if she knew the ritual way he removed or did not remove his clothing, she greeted him and his wife, his mother, his children as she did any slight acquaintance on the street, in the shops, at festivals, at the post office.

After one visit, Handra did not return to the States; she rarely wrote letters; she ordered fewer books, then none at all. Michelle and Clive shrugged when asked and said she'd "disappeared north of nowhere." When heavy winds whipped away a section of her roof and rains rendered her passport unreadable, Handra tossed it into the fire. If she recalled her life in the states, images of fans and leaf blowers intruded. In the stillness of her cottage and among the stones, she connected body and universe. She spent her days dealing with winds, storms, rain, sunshine, mastering weaving and dyeing, tending lost lambs and men.

From the beginning, it was understood that money was not part of any transaction between Handra and the men of the island. Theirs was not a commercial enterprise, this giving and taking. They would not have used the term spiritual activity; no, it was highly physical; they marveled at her stamina; they marveled at their own. But there was something indefinably different in the activity in Handra's cottage and in their own--or surely they would not have found their way there. Handra said very little; in time, she said less. Perhaps each man in his heart wanted her to cry out, to tell him in words how he was doing, how she was feeling, but none asked her and she did not say. If they enjoyed a cup of tea or coffee afterwards, sitting at the tiny

25

kitchen table, the man might talk of the weather, the crops, his wife's illness; Handra listened, nodding occasionally. "Is the chimney drawing well, then?" Alex might inquire, taking a pipe from his pocket, tamping the tobacco. "Any thing I can fix up for you?" "The chimney's perfect now," Handra might reply, not adding that George had seen to that. "The wheel's in need of a tack or two to sturdy it." Soon the spinning wheel was in perfect working order. A tip of Alex's hat and he was gone.

Handra went often to the stones at night; among the shadows, in the darkness if no moon shone, she sat or lay, still, matching her breathing to the rhythms of the earth. She was aware that others knew she frequented the stones. Perhaps they whispered; perhaps they wondered. She knew that sometimes she breathed in tandem with the earth, and when she must arise, bones protesting, joints sometimes cracking, her breath became jagged for a time until she readjusted to a vertical stance. And if the moon was especially bright, Handra felt warmed, smiled upon. On the coldest of nights she did not shiver even as her breath showed white in the air. Outside the circle, pedaling strongly, then she felt the icy air, felt the moisture crystalize in her throat. Then she was glad to return to the fire-warmth of the cottage. Sometimes someone had been there, had stoked the fire, had brought in peat and coal. If a visitor found the cottage empty, though, he did not stay, did not wait for Handra. That would have been imposing.

Handra was a healthy woman, unhampered by colds or allergies, but she was not invincible. When her bike hit a bit of debris on the dark road, she flew over the handlebars and broke her right arm. Steering with one hand and ignoring the sweat pouring into her eyes, she managed to get to her cottage. Luckily Jack arrived the next morning as the sun rose and took her to the nearest clinic. Over the next few days, Jack's grown daughter and other women helped Handra with chores, wiped her face when she perspired in pain, left food for her; they also of course took the opportunity to study the cottage— to compliment Handra's designs and craftsmanship, the muted shades of some yarn, the savage hues of others. If a husband was familiar with the layout of the cottage he did not indicate it in the presence of his wife, allowing her to step before him into the front room, to find her own way to the kitchen. Handra let herself be cared for and expressed simple wonder and gratitude at their kindnesses. Her eyes, whale-gray, solemn, were clear and direct.

"If I didn't know it for a fact," Ellen Guise said to her friend, "I couldn't look at her and believe--believe what we know to be true."

Her friend sipped the brandy-warmed coffee and considered "the woman of the stones." "It's a mystery," she concluded. The women did not discuss Handra in any depth or at length because what was there to say. Nothing she did changed the outward flow of life on the island; if what she did changed the inward flow, who could determine that for sure? A comment here and there about Handra and then silence. Not one woman could honestly claim she'd lost a man because of Handra; not one could say she had lost a "mating" because of her. Were the husbands and lovers kinder, gentler, more knowledgeable following their visits? The women weren't saying. And the men said nothing. How could they know, then, that Handra allowed no heavy drinkers in her cottage? How did they know not to go there stinking of alcohol? How was it generally known that only one man had been turned away at the door for no reason that they could see--or smell. Yet it was known that Henry Muese stood at Handra's door one afternoon, was spoken to, and turned away, never to return. He had old, sad eyes, yes, the island knew that, but only he knew what Handra referred to when she took his hands in hers and said quietly, "There's too much, too much, too dark. No." Only Henry, not Handra, not his middle-aged daughter, knew that Henry's hands had operated the levers at gas chambers in another country and that Henry's eyes could never forget that work.

So Handra lived quietly, weaving, walking, growing ageless in the stillness. She seldom spoke after her fiftieth year, yet she radiated calm contentment. Her body grew slightly stouter, her face remained smooth and unwrinkled. Her hair threaded with gray. She seemed as natural a part of the environment as the sea, the stones, the green pastures, the pathways. She seemed at peace.

On the night of November 7, a clear night, clear and cold, Handra closed the door of her cottage and walked the half mile to the coast. She wore her usual black pants, black jacket and heavy boots. The sea was as calm as it ever was. Handra looked until she found what she must have hidden there earlier: two very heavy stones. She placed them in her jacket, knotted her belt around them so they must remain in place, and then she walked into the sea. Far, far down the narrow coastline, young Alex was driving a wandering bullock home, he flicking a switch at it, the bullock swishing its tail, neither in any hurry. Alex saw the dark shape cutting into the sea against the sky, already so far out that he didn't countenance what he thought he saw. He saw hands white, reaching skyward, stretched up toward the moon. Then the silhouette disappeared. Alex stared, ran toward the spot, looked again. Nothing. He ran to the nearest cottage-- Handra's--and when he found it empty, neat, tidied up, he knew what he had seen.

The sergeant found, not a note, but a torn piece of newspaper. It announced what the islanders had all read days before--salvaging operations were being undertaken to dredge a nearby area where a seventh-century ship was believed to have gone down. The article described the mammoth equipment needed for the task--and those who stood in Handra's cottage had heard that morning the monotonous whirring of engines, droning, whining, sucking away at the sea, sucking away the silence.

Topless in Estoril

I could go topless in Estoril, Maewee thought, looking at a woman whose swimsuit top lay discarded in the sand. Still groggy from her flight to Lisbon and the wild ride to the hotel (the driver, she was sure, sought to impress her with his whipping around slower traffic, his nonchalant one-handed control of the limo, and with her tip she had smilingly obliged him by thanking him and whooshing her hand through the air), she sipped the dark coffee, wondering if she could manage three sips from the minute serving. She shrugged, tossed the strong liquid down, almost gagged, and motioned for another. What she really wanted, under the layers of tourist behavior she did not intend to exhibit, was a steaming cup of McDonald's brew in a paper cup, fragrant and familiar...and large enough to savor for more than forty-five seconds. The waiter placed another tiny cup before her.

"*Obrigado*" she said, practicing the one word she'd learned of Portugese, one she'd seen on several huge billboards along the highway from the airport.

"*Obrigada*, madam," the waiter said. "If one is woman speaking, *obrigada*. Man," he gestured to his chest, "is *obrigado*."

"Oh. *Obrigada*, then," Maewee said. In the country less than two hours and already a lesson in grammar. She returned to her viewing.

The woman was big, not obese, but stout. Her stomach muscles had long since relaxed and rolled with gravity, and so had her breasts. She wore a reasonably cut bottom of a swim suit, not high cut, and some cellulite streaks were faintly visible. Topless, the woman appeared indifferent to the few people on the beach and to the cafe patrons who sat on the elevated stone esplanade that ran along the coast. A small red plastic bucket sat beside the chaise lounge and occasionally she cupped her hand into it and threw splashes of water on her torso and legs. Once she delicately sprinkled drops on her toes before again reclining. Maewee studied the other people on the beach, an assortment unlikely to be seen at Myrtle Beach or Atlantic City or even (though what did she know of that?) along the Big Sur: a woman lay slightly curled, up close to the esplanade, her head on a magazine, her body enclosed entirely in black; a naked toddler cavorted farther down the beach, squealing as it approached the sea; a couple seemed asleep, their faces turned toward each other but not touching; at the jetty several teenage boys dove repeatedly into the sea and climbed laboriously up the rocks to drip and dive again; two older men, barefoot, in rolled up trousers batted a ball back and forth, and a lone dog nosed its way through the sand. Everything seemed in slow motion, lazy.

Maewee's eyes returned to the woman. Such utter indifference to those around her. Or was it utter assimilation with those around her. Maewee pondered the scene. If the woman had been beautiful, with legs long and sensual, if her breasts had been firm, jaunty, would she have attracted attention, envy, dreams, condemnation? A longing as tangible as hunger filled Maewee, a longing not for the body (hers was similar in every visible way) but for the freedom to be so unaware of both body and strangers.

Two weeks ago when the congregation--not strangers--sent out cold waves of condemnation followed by silent nods or averted glances, Maewee knew she had to get away from Havers Memorial Church and Haverston itself. The pastor was conveniently absent that Sunday, it being the annual state convention time. The pastor was part of the problem, but the congregation might, *might* forgive him but not the woman they considered his seducer.

30

Of course, Pastor Jarvis was married. The Haverston church would never have hired an unmarried minister, especially one who was past the prime marrying time. They accepted his explanation: "My wife's staying in Arkansas for a few months. Her mother's Alzheimers is getting worse. Her dad's failing...." The congregation met Mrs. Jarvis only once in the ten months of the Reverend's ministry. A woman accompanied him to church one Sunday, stayed at the parsonage three days, helped him with grocery shopping one day, and returned, he said, to Arkansas, sorry that she hadn't entertained anyone, worn out from constant caregiving and the quick trip to see her husband, and confirm his marital status.

"Shy, she was," Mrs. Barton, who had met her, pronounced.

"Or uppity," Mrs. Smythe, who hadn't met her, said.

But, at least, the congregation's doubts, if doubts they were, were appeased. There was a Mrs. Jarvis. She was pretty, young enough to still be shy, dark-haired and hazel-eyed like her husband, the same intonation--well-bred Arkansas.

Maewee had been married once, so long ago it seemed and so briefly that she hardly remembered the details of the eight months. Andrew Bolton Carstairs. She'd loved his name and later after the divorce she joked about learning the ABC's of sex from him. For a time her friends asked if she'd heard anything from The Alphabet. But the joke palled; the memory faded into a kind of never-never land. She wondered if Andy could have been as blond, as fair, as beautiful, slim, shining as she remembered. Surely not. At any rate, he was long since dead: a water skiing accident. In his mid-thirties, he had insisted on skiing as an eighteen-year old might and had lost control in a tricky maneuver...so she heard. When he was, in fact, nineteen, he had seemed experienced beyond his years and she had flirted outrageously with him, as had the other girls just graduated from high school and working at Camp Tekota. Why he had singled her out was a mystery to her then and still to her acquaintances; she was not the slimmest, not the most beautiful, not the most clever. Perhaps she was the most worshiping, adoring him with large brown eyes, flushing at his slightest notice, willing to give her body, her virginity--everything if only he asked.

They eloped on her eighteenth birthday, and she intended to be a model wife. She set out to make him happy and immediately she determined to lose weight. She drank water, she made herself vomit, she skipped meals. She became pale. She fainted one day. Andy went to college and worked part time; she worked full time and starved herself. Their lovemaking was energetic and yet dream-like. She couldn't remember most of it, but the joints they shared may have contributed to her sensation of rushing waters, cawing birds, and buttered popcorn. An analyst would have said the rushing water and the popcorn could be explained by her job with the Metropolitan Sewage Board and Andy's job managing the concession stand at MiraMovies; even the ceaseless squawking of the blackbirds might be explained by the occasional blasts of the neighbor's ham radio. One night, Andy roused himself to look at her. "You're thin as a slat," he said. And he didn't look happy.

As Andy grew more distant, Maewee grew thinner, worrying about why he didn't hold her, why he turned aside, why he hardly brushed her cheek when he came home, why he came home later and tireder. He had introduced her to sex and then seemed to lose interest. After a friend reported seeing him with a dark hefty girl, after another friend swore she saw him with a plump, braided-blonde Swedish exchange student, even after she saw him leaving the theater (she sat in the parking lot) with a heavy, dark-haired girl, Maewee didn't catch on quickly. She just grew hollow-eyed and gaunt. Andy's mother called several days after he disappeared; she sounded weepy and confused but determined to support her son.

"He's getting a quick divorce, he says to tell you. You can keep everything in the apartment, and the lease is not up for three months." Maewee heard her mother-in-law take a deep breath. "We've sent a check to cover the rent for those months. It's not your fault, Mary Marie. His daddy says to tell you it's not your fault."

Maewee gained her weight back; she moped around the apartment and she moped around her job until finally she was fired. Then she drank Diet Cokes and ate pink Snowballs for two solid weeks. Her few friends despaired. One day she pulled herself together, washed her hair, and went to the local branch of the state university; she began studying biology, specializing in marine life. Janie, her former co-worker, asked her what suddenly happened. "I woke up burping on a Monday morning and thought to myself: I can lie here and burp the rest of my life or I can get up and do something. Biology's the only class that wasn't full when I registered late."

Maewee finished her degree, took education courses and became a teacher, returned to a county thirty miles from her home, and saw the ocean only twice a year. She settled in to becoming "The Best Teacher of the Year," attending prom nights and chaperoning various groups, able to fill in at the last moment when other teachers had dates, weddings, parties. The assumption always was that Maewee would be free. For twenty- five years she layered social obligations, school functions, and club meetings into her life, so that by external icing she could push the kernel of self further and further from the surface. Her students called her Miss Mae and her friends--for she had many--called her what a three-year old neighbor boy had christened her--Maewee. When Mary Marie asked her parents why in the world they had given her both names, her mother had the slight grace to look embarrassed and her father had simply turned back to his wrestling magazine. They hadn't been able to agree when it was time to name the baby: her mother wanted Mary Wilton (after her family name) and her father had opted for (in his opinion) the more sophisticated Marie James (his father's name). They had spoken simultaneously and so she had started life, she thought, as a redundancy. Secretly she thanked the little boy for her name, especially when she saw that her parents shuddered each time someone used it.

The town of Haverston expected, she was told and she learned, certain behaviors of its teachers and those who stayed the course and retired from the system adjusted their private and public lives accordingly. As long as the private didn't intrude noticeably into the public, little attention was given to individual foibles (private) or character flaws (when they became public). That Marvin Struggs stayed married to his invalid and nagging wife was admirable; that he spent much of her money and his time in motels down at the beach with girls who waited tables at the Cowboy Lounge was ignored. Mrs. Jeffries--like clockwork--went on an alcoholic binge every three months and had to take some personal leave days to sober up, but she was a topnotch home economics. teacher who could sew a fine seam, make exquisite puff pastries, and preside over the annual Beta Club Banquet--as long as it was scheduled around her binge-time. The new teachers who, of course, were usually young and inexperienced either quickly learned to cover any unapproved habits or they decided to leave for greener pastures. Cute Ms. Shepherd should never have bought pot from a semi-local boy whose aunt ran Ruthie's Hair Salon. And young Leon Harris should have known better than to go out with--much less be seen with his pants down in the backseat of his old sedan by teenage boys who envied him his lush mustache and long hair--the Sampson twins. Maewee survived by doing good and being good--and assuring herself she was happy.

Twenty-five years without sex? Hardly. The vice-principal had needed consoling after his mother's death while his wife was temporarily away; Maewee took a casserole and stayed no longer than neighbors might assume any duty call would take. When the wife returned, Maewee said goodby to him in his office. The door was closed and the coupling was quick and efficient, so efficient that the vice-principal gasped, "We can't stop seeing each other...I need you. Don't leave me." Maewee regretted her loss, too, but how many casseroles could she deliver and how many times could a school problem demand a closed door, and, she thought later, how rehearsed his words sounded. She adjusted her clothes and said, "No. It's over."

She could count her lovers on the fingers of one hand, she mused; her one regret was the senior officer at her bank. Try though she did and try though he did, their affair was little more than attempts; perhaps only she--and his estranged wife--knew of his failures at love. When he drove into a bridge abutment one day after work, the town poured out sympathy for his wife and admiration for his financial brilliance.

Maewee was a graceful woman, moving easily in her flowing two-piece dresses, wearing low heels so she never tottered. She smiled easily, she appeared genuinely touched by small tokens from her students and friends, she supplied conversation at dinner parties when an extra was needed, and she drank only in the company of others, never alone. Perhaps she feared the loss of inhibition that might accompany alcohol; perhaps she thought her smile might falter, her good will might fail, her dark side might illumine her bland countenance.

For gradually--or had it simply appeared?--a festering irritation at her own restrictions, her chosen constraints, began to prick at her solid behaviors. She itched one day to snap at Mrs. Richardson at the farmers' market when she insisted on detailing the growth of the asparagus from seed to stalk; she wanted to close her ears to yet another excuse for poor work from yet another student who had missed lab and class for whatever good reason. The long compressed sand of her being was stirred as if disturbed by an unseen giant propeller. She smiled at her own metaphor. Of course, she knew it was connected to hormones, to her age, a very natural process; but surely it was more than that: this being aware that her emotions had expanded to almost the bursting point; her flesh pushed against her skin at the slightest provocation (and comments, scenes, all part of the usual environment seemed provocation). The mirror showed that she looked no different; she hadn't gained nor lost weight.

Why, then, this sense of imminent explosion? Some months into this state she took a satchel of materials back to the minister, books a Sunday school teacher had borrowed and then left with Maewee to return when she was suddenly transferred to Minneapolis.

Mr. Jarvis opened the door cautiously, she thought, but then regarded her with relief. He had a glass of white wine in the hand which finally came from behind his back and beckoned her into the room. "Come in, Ms., Miss Mary," he almost stammered. "You caught me with my evening 'constitutional,' as they say. Would you like a glass of something?"

"Just diet cola," Maewee said. As he went toward the kitchen, she called, "No, I'll have a glass of whatever you're drinking." She put the books on a hall table and sat down.

He returned with his glass replenished and a glass for her along with a paper plate of cheese and crackers. "It's Crackerbarrel," he said. "But the wine is good. My indulgence, you might say."

Maewee explained her errand and sipped her wine. He seemed edgy, she thought, although he attempted some enthusiasm about the various activities in the church. Finally she said, "What's wrong, Mr. Jarvis? Have I come at a bad time?" She shifted her weight in the soft chair.

"No, no. It's not a bad time," he said. Then a nervous giggle escaped. "A bad time... right now, anytime's a bad time."

"I don't understand." Maewee's thoughts were turned toward escape; she gulped her wine and set the glass on the end table between them. It was not as if she and Mr. Jarvis were friends, not as if she knew enough about the church to recognize if there were problems. A shock ran through her when he put his hand, cold from the wine he'd been cradling, over hers. She stiffened and he immediately removed his hand.

"Sorry about that," he said. "I, I guess I need some company right now. Can you stay awhile?"

"Well, sure, if you're sure, I mean..." They were both

stuttering like teenagers. Maewee settled back into the chair, the scene of seduction that flashed across her mind gone the moment he stood up.

"Call me Thad, would you?" He went toward the kitchen. "I'm heating a casserole somebody brought and I'll get us some more wine." He turned. "Chicken casserole, appropriate enough."

Maewee could have speculated about what he had to talk about. She'd listened so long and so often, though, to her students' confidences and to those of her friends that she simply tuned out speculation and looked around at the parsonage. The room was neat; fresh flowers sat on the mantel, a collection of Lladro occupied shelves near the stereo equipment. Whatever she might have speculated about Mr. Jarvis's--Thad's--situation, it was not what he announced.

"I'm not really married. I persuaded my sister to come visit that time," he said. They were finishing the bottle of wine and Maewee's stomach growled as the fragrance of the chicken casserole drifted from the kitchen.

"Why? Why didn't you just say you weren't married?"

"You know how churches are," he said. "They'd be wondering about every woman in the congregation." He had relaxed considerably since her arrival and his legs sprawled out comfortably before him. He made a teepee with his fingers. "I'm not inclined toward marriage, Mary Marie."

"Oh."

"I'm going to have to decide," he closed his eyes and went on, "I'm going to have to decide whether to stay in the church, given the views, given the views..." He couldn't seem to finish.

Maewee looked at his hands, his closed eyes, his eyelashes slightly dark against his face, the red spots where his glasses, which he'd taken off, pinched his nose. She understood what he couldn't say. She helped him out.

"The conference voted last year, you know," she said. "And even if--well, regardless of what the national organization might someday say, Haverston wouldn't stand for it."

"God, I know it. I thought I could manage. I really thought I could pull it off. This is only my second church, you know. Cynthia agreed to visit so I could postpone making a decision." He pulled his legs up, put his elbows on his knees and said, "But Bill, Bill's not going to wait; he's issued an ultimatum. Right after conference next month, I have to choose: him or the church." Maewee poured the rest of the bottle of wine into his glass. And waited.

"We could live in Chicago. He's got a job there, could get me one. Believe me, Mary Marie, I have prayed and prayed, but nothing is settled."

"Though I have wept and fasted, wept and prayed and seen my head brought in upon a platter," Maewee muttered. "That's T.S. Eliot." She stood up, weaving only slightly. "Let's eat."

During dinner they talked of other things, and Maewee thought she should leave when they cleared the table. But Thad insisted on digging among the pantry until he found a bottle of Bailey's Irish Cream. "Cynthia brought it when she came," he said. And they were back to his dilemma. By eleven o'clock and more Baileys and then instant coffee, Thad was weeping openly. Maewee went to sit beside him on the sofa and folded her arms around him, drawing his head to her shoulder. She comforted him as a mother might, stroking his hair, feeling slightly drunk and slightly foolish as he sobbed against her bosom. In fact, she must have reminded him of his mother. "Mama never believed it...I tried while I was in seminary to tell her. She wouldn't believe it. She said 'just because you were raised in a house with women'... she said I had a choice...she said Daddy'd die twice if it was true. I stopped talking about it. I dated a few girls."

If they hadn't had too much wine, they--surely one of them--would have thought to close the blinds. They didn't and Mrs. Anderson's bridge club ladies all passed the house on their way to the corner lot where they had parked their cars. So not just one woman saw the scene, but seven...and all interpreted it in one way.

Maewee was vaguely aware of some sort of surveillance, but she certainly couldn't turn her head. Her blouse was damp and she was weary, so in a few minutes she gently pushed Thad away and said she had to go. At the door he blew his nose and tried to apologize, but suddenly they both hiccuped loudly. They giggled and hugged and she agreed to let him take her to dinner on Friday night. "I'll behave," he said. "I owe you a good dinner for listening to me."

And so before Thad Jarvis came back from the church's annual conference, Maewee finished the school year and realized what the congregation assumed, realized further that she could not tell the truth, and realized further that she could do nothing to help Thad with his choice. Like Keats when he knew he was dying, she departed for a sunnier clime.

Three days later, Maewee sat looking at the beach, shaded by the white and blue table umbrella. A glass of *vinho verde* sweated in front of her; the Atlantic lay calm as a sleeping snail blue and almost motionless. Maewee knew that under that serene surface teemed millions upon millions of live creatures, darting, devouring, slithering, tearing at each other, holding on, watchful, waiting, moving constantly to stay alive. It was a dangerous place, underwater. Yet, the surface gleamed with a blue, heavenly serenity. Her biologist's knowledge of the nature of existence didn't destroy the sense of peacefulness she felt, sitting alone, surrounded by tourists and a few locals, sipping and munching...crunching between their teeth some of those creatures from the sea. She had been like a sea creature, she mused, creating a shell for protection, a shell of flesh, a shell of behaviors. And she had survived. Now she determined to live.

"I could go topless in Estoril," she said.

She smiled at an Englishman who walked by. He had

tipped his hat to her the day before. He would join her if she smiled again. Before that, though, she had to buy a two-piece bathing suit–and maybe a little plastic bucket.

The Grand Canal

The sun of the early April morning shimmered on the Grand Canal and shimmered too on the white neck of Adrian Whitfield as she leaned back in the wooden chair. For a moment she forgot to think of the proximity of her purse and other persons (the tourist literature was so very explicit about not being a prey); for a moment she forgot why she was here. For the moment she basked, long-legged, pale-faced, black-haired, in simply being. Had a passerby asked "being what?" she could not have answered with any certainty.

She had arrived by plane and train, at Venice in a twilight of mist four days ago; a vaporetto had been her means of transport to near the hotel she'd phoned from Milano. Deposited at Academia Station, Adrian carried her two small bags to San Stephano Square, easy enough to find with her tourist map. Checking the directions again, she saw the flower stall on the corner, turned as directed, walked too far, returned to the flower stall to point to the hotel name and said, "*Dove?*" to the man closing up.

He emerged from behind the flowers, walked a few steps and pointed. "Hotel Locanda Fiora" he said in such a liquid voice that tears came to her eyes. Perhaps he saw them in the lamplight, for he asked, "Okay?" She nodded and crossed the small, deserted square to the hotel. The desk clerk, noting her weariness, with gestures and a few words in English told her a hot drink and a roll would be available at a small table in the corridor in a few minutes. Adrian practiced her second word of Italian, "*Grazie.*" Then she slept for fourteen hours.

Su Wan's fortune cookies had determined her destination. "*Water dreams await you.*" She thought that didn't make sense, so she tore open the plastic and broke another cookie. Su Wan always brought her two cookies at his China Kingdom. She had consumed a platter of sesame chicken, hot rice and green tea as she tried to think of her next step. The second cookie told her: "*Seek water--find true fortune.*" She mused as she nibbled. Water surely meant more than nearby Lake Mocassee, perhaps even the Atlantic. A vision of Venice floated across her consciousness, a Venice of a travel poster three doors down in MacKenzie's Travel Agency. Why not? "Fortune's smiling on you," Mr. MacK told her--when she showed him the cookie slips. "A fantastic twenty-one day special. Now's the time to go."

Adrian walked for hours every day. She sampled each square she found, resting and sunning, letting the locals and the tourists flow around her. At bridge after bridge she looked into the depths of the canals, soon not noticing the plastic bottles, the litter, the orange peels eddying around the edges. The dark waters occasionally sent up dank and rotting, sewage smells. She usually carried a hydrangea, and bent her nostrils to it if the odors intruded. Franco at the flower stand had given her the flower the first morning as she tentatively wandered from her hotel. He waved her lire aside with a slight bow. Today the surly pink hydrangea lay across her lap, wilting slightly.

Each day brought some new delight; the city's palette of color, both vibrant and pastel, opened her senses to herself. Adrian began to indulge in choices without thinking of what Harold or her mother might have said. She disliked sitting in molded plastic chairs, for example, and sought out cafes without them. She stopped wearing lipstick. She disliked roses, so when Franco bowed on the second morning and offered her a long stemmed yellow rose, she smiled and shook her head. Her eyes turned from the rose to the hydrangeas...and he gallantly took one from its water can.

On this fourth day, she had held her hand before her, the small diamond glittering in the as-yet pale sunlight. The temptation had been great to plunk it into the murky canal over which she earlier had leaned on the Calle Stagneri; a waft of rankness drifted up from the waters.

Instead she marched into a touristy gift shop nearby. There she took off the engagement ring and traded it for thousands of lire and an outrageous metal elephant necklace on a heavy chain. The shopkeeper shrugged eloquently at his good fortune and Adrian walked away with the necklace and a lighter step. Back at Piazza San Marco she bought a frothy cappuccino and extended her hand, willing the whiteness on her ring finger to disappear in the Venetian sunlight.

Perhaps something showed in her face, for a handsome well-dressed tourist indicated the empty table and asked in German-accented English, "May I join you?" She shook her head. Within a few minutes a gondolier in blue shirt, black pants and striped neck scarf offered to sit beside her. She assumed indifference and said, "No, no, I wait." With a flourish of his straw hat and a flashing display of beautiful teeth, he left her. Draping her light sweater across another chair she lay her head back to accept the sunlight.

She allowed the lightness of her left hand to travel up her arm, following its journey in her mind; she felt it enter her shoulder blades, like clear water finding its way upward, then down past the elephant necklace indenting her shirt, accenting her breasts. Like an interior bathing, the delicious sense of freedom moved into her thighs, down her calves, entered her toes. It was a moment of sheer sensation unlinked to thought. Had thoughts flowed with the senses, they would have been questions: Why did I wait so long? Why did I feel bound so long by a ring and a promise whispered in an airport lounge?

Her mother had dismissed Harold as lightly as she dismissed Adrian's college dreams of majoring in art. "Study for an education degree," she'd advised. "You'll always be able to get a job. Do you know any sculptors or water colorists who make a living at it?" Adrian, trained from birth to pay attention to her mother's decrees, thought about it and concluded that, once again, her mother was right.

"The man's unreliable," her mother said when Adrian returned from seeing Harold off at the airport. His destination was Los Angeles; his expectation was a job in a newly created electronics company. Adrian's expectation was that he would return within six months and take her from Nosegay, Indiana, and her exhausting job at the elementary school.

"Mother, we're engaged. He's going to get settled. Then he'll be back and we'll arrange the wedding." Adrian was then twenty-six, slightly plump, and eager to please...whether it was her mother's dictates or Harold's demands.

"Any man can put a diamond on a girl's finger..." Mrs. Whitfield paused so that Adrian could be in doubt as to her meaning, "...for whatever reason." She whipped the blanket around her thin knees. "I don't trust a man who doesn't have family somewhere. Chicago--shhmagno. We'll see."

Two phone calls, two postcards, and six years later, Adrian still wore the ring. The years wound themselves around her as insidiously as strands of ivy creeping, growing, covering and smothering the daffodils and lilies in their garden. At her mother's insistence, Adrian tried to trace Harold, but Chicago and Los Angeles were the only cities she could connect him to, and in neither was a Harold Sorenson found. As she waited, Adrian grew thin. The hollows of her cheekbones gave her face a gaunt, almost a saintly look. As she waited, Adrian cared for her mother who in her fifties developed a multitude of problems, culminating in emphysema and oxygen tanks. As she waited, Adrian more and more declined the gradually declining invitations from her circle of friends; her mother's friends became her friends and she became their errand girl. "Adrian can take you to the doctor," Mrs. Whitfield would declare. "She's not busy after she gets home from school."

In the attitude of her mother and her mother's friends, Adrian sensed that somehow she was at fault in Harold's not returning. Had she been more assertive, had she been more acquiescent, had she been more clever, less virginal...they surely all had their views on what she could have done. She had not a clue. She had met Harold in a school supply store when she bought materials for a Halloween bulletin board. He was looking for a new fountain pen. With her help, he chose an elegant, slim Waterman. They went next door to drink coffee, a safe enough proposition, she was sure.

As often as she reviewed their first and subsequent meetings, as many times as Adrian relived those fevered hours in his hotel room, she could see no indication of deception in his intense blue eyes, his declaring voice. Before he left, when his consulting job concluded at Rafton Industries, they slept together every afternoon in the last week, the week he presented her with the engagement ring and the announcement that he'd be flying to the west coast. Harold was the only man she'd slept with, the only man she'd actually been in bed with, even if they never slept out the night together. She was sure she loved him, but perhaps she loved only the urging hands, the demanding lips, the sense of totally giving, of being almost obliterated by his need. Still, in those first years as she waited, she assumed that his need would return him to her; she expected she would spend her life waiting for his hands on her white skin.

As Mrs. Whitfield's condition consumed more and more of her daughter's life, the memory of Harold dimmed somewhat. A wariness kept Adrian's eyes from signaling any approachability; a slight tightness developed around her mouth. Each time her mother called for her an involuntary muscle contraction occurred. To compensate, Adrian painted her lips a glowing mauve. She wore the same lipstick year after year.

One afternoon as Adrian deposited supplies in the corner of the principal's office, she heard Melanie, who taught two doors down, say, "It'll be a relief when her bitch of a mother dies."

"It may be too late by then, the way she's going," responded an older teacher.

Adrian wanted to smash her fist against the wall--at the realization that people, especially her friend Melanie, discussed her, at the realization that she agreed with the astute Mrs. Blanssom. After feeding her mother that night, Adrian devoured plate after plate of sweet and sour pork at the China Kingdom. Su Wan came over to her table. "Missy okay? Missy fine?" Adrian wiped red sticky sauce from her lips and assured him she was fine. Over the years he had recognized the symptoms, the hunger, that brought her to his table, so he ventured to pat her shoulder lightly and retreated behind his cash register.

Three months after she heard the friends talking, Adrian was shaking their hands at her mother's funeral. She detected nothing other than sympathy in their words and warm hands. Melanie said, "Come over for lunch on Saturday. We'll talk." Adrian felt as if she'd been hollowed out and a wooden core inserted into her being. It kept her standing straight, upright. There was no surprise in her mother's dying. Mrs. Whitfield's last words to her daughter were a croaked, raspy, "Be here tomorrow by eleven." The hospital had called at 3:30 a.m. She knew her mother was dead then, but she rushed as if she might have one more glimpse of her papery face alive. She received the doctors' words and the nurse's commiseration with an oaken calm, collected the few items from her mother's room, and drove home again.

After her private mourning, Adrian was prepared to go through the motions of her mother's departure. The minister dwelt on the love and care Adrian had given her mother, that a daughter could give so much added value to the mother, a mother who could inspire such devotion. A newcomer to Nosegay, the Reverend Masters had seen Mrs. Whitfield only in the hospital; he assumed Adrian would attend church once she was not needed at home. Adrian thanked him, paid him, and promised nothing.

When she surveyed the potato salad, the cakes, the deviled eggs that friends had sent, she wanted fried rice, noodles, sweet and sour pork, crispy chicken coated with sesame seeds. Su Wan's nephew, who spoke English flawlessly, called. "Uncle is sending food to you, Miss Whitfield. The boy will deliver within twenty minutes." He hesitated, "Unless you'd rather not. Uncle is at this moment filling containers." Adrian could only manage, "Oh yes, please. Thank your uncle. Thank you."

Now Adrian had time-- "as much time as you need" her principal had told her. "But you will be back in the fall?" She also had a house and car in Nosegay and decisions to make.

In the following days, Adrian roamed the city and then sat facing the Grand Canal. She chose to ignore the museums, the churches, the palaces, the history of the city, preferring the sensual to the historical understanding. Once, though, she picked up a discarded pamphlet describing the Campanile on her left. The ancient tower had one day simply fallen, incredibly injuring no one, and even more incredibly, was then rebuilt "on the same spot and on the same design."

The sunlight on the canals, the pink lamplight in the streets at dusk, the strangeness of the watery city, the enveloping ease with which she adopted its *calii* and waterways--these lures tempted her...to live the expatriate life, to discard all that she could of responsibilities. She had to do more, after all, than discard a ring that so anchored her heart. Walking or resting, again and again, she caressed the necklace, warm in the sunlight, slightly rough in construction. Her fingers followed the curves until she knew even the tiny indentations marking the elephant's feet, its toenails. Someone had fashioned the shape, some fingers, trained or untrained, some time, in some workshop, had used flame and craft to dare to create...to create...the word floated on the wings of the sea gulls circling close. The glinting, fluttery luminescence of their wings jarred her vision.

The next day, in a dusty shop corner, Adrian found a paint box and a dozen brushes. Almost fearfully she laid out the materials on her bed. Her first dippings and strokes were tentative. Then she swirled the brush around to capture the curlicues of the milky blue hydrangea stuck in a vase on her bedside table. Three hours later, Adrian put aside her brush and paper, rubbed her eyes, and filled the electric kettle with water for a cup of tea. She resolved not to inspect her first effort until the morning.

For two days, Adrian stayed in her room, drinking hot tea, eating dry rolls. In those long hours she rediscovered the techniques she'd mastered in freshman art classes. With intense concentration, she rearranged the bedside lamp until it satisfied her with its glow and reflections on the objects she painted: the drooping flower, her teacups, her necklace, the buttons along her jacket. Noting the slant of the late afternoon sun shafting through the window, she draped the lacy curtain to diffuse it against the bedside table. She did not want to attempt to capture the fading pastels, the pinks, oranges, greens of the palaces and facades until she felt ready; it would be a sort of desecration. She hardly stopped to sleep. The hotel night manager came to her room the second night, tapping lightly.

"Are you all right, Miss Whitfield?" Her English was halting. "I bring these for you." She proffered a small basket filled with an apple, a banana, two oranges, and small packaged pastries.

Adrian grinned, yellow paint on her cheek, her fingers stained, her t-shirt soiled, her hair a mess.

"Gosh, thank you, Signora. *Grazie.* I am hungry!" She placed the basket on the table, already considering how she might capture its texture. "I forget about eating. Will you join me? I can make tea."

The woman said, "*Non, grazie.*" She hesitated.

"Franco, Franco at the flowers...he ask about you."

"Tell him I'm fine," Adrian said. "No, I will see him tomorrow." She picked up the wilted hydrangea. "I need a new one," she said. She and the manager giggled like schoolgirls and the manager said, "Good night, then. I go."

Adrian, scrubbed and glowing, emerged from the hotel the next morning to greet Franco when he arrived at the flower stall. His eyes lit up and his dog Dante rubbed against her leg. "I'll take him for a walk before my breakfast is ready," she announced. Franco brought the old collie almost every day and the dog slept in a broken orange chair in the sun, only occasionally blinking if a group of boisterous children came by. She and Dante had taken several walks together; Dante seemed equally happy to sun for hours or to pace sedately beside Adrian along the canals and down the alleys. Franco tipped his cap and pointed to his freshly cut hydrangeas, today creamy blue and white. He looked so solid, so kind she resisted an impulse to hug him.

The rains descended later that day and Adrian experienced the city with water above and water below. In the blinding frenzy, buildings blurred, streets flowed. Fuzzily, lines from a poem came to her: "clouds upon clouds above me, waste upon waste beneath" which surely she was paraphrasing, but she remembered clearly the last line: "I cannot, will not go." Whatever had kept Emily Bronte caught in the poem had escaped Adrian in a long-ago lit class, but the poem's line teased her now as she stood only partially shielded by a doorway. She stepped into the rain and walked to the shop with Internet access, easier than locating a bookstore with Bronte's poems in English. "A tyrant spell has bound me..." Reading the poem on the screen left Adrian in the same uncertainty as in her sophomore class, but it triggered a very different impulse in her. "I can go now," she thought. She said aloud, "I will, I will go..."

Leaving the shop in the downpour, she spread her arms wide, raised her face to welcome the drenching, shrugged her head from its rain scarf and let the rain plaster her dark hair against her neck and face. Tears may have mingled with the rain, for her eyes were shining. Through the maze of streets, she couldn't see it but she knew the Campanile stood rebuilt and strong. It would be too easy to adhere to Venice, to be captured by its light, to be captivated by its charm, to be, perhaps in time, loved by one or more of its men. The few people hurrying by or huddling against walls under awnings looked at her as if she were demented-- skipping, hardly dodging the puddles, waving her arms, welcoming the rain. *Back to Indiana*, she shouted to herself. *Nosegay, here I come!*

The Cat

Marie stared at the TV screen, but she saw the black cat. Sometimes sleek, sometimes Persian-bushy, always stark black, the cat popped before her eyes at the weirdest times.

For three days this had been so. The first time, she was driving down the interstate on her way to visit her mother, luckily recovering after surgery, when the cat had floated across her windshield and melted out the corner like recent ice. Except the wind had long since dried the window. The cat had simply oozed away and she jerked her attention from the edge of the window back to the road, helped by a trucker's horn reminding her she'd strayed left of the centerline. Her mind on her mother, Marie hadn't taken much notice of the image except to wonder, "What brought that on?"

The next time, Marie was absently chewing a blueberry muffin in the company cafeteria, absently too reading the comics in the daily paper, and absently saying "Hi" to someone who passed her table. The cat, minute as a thumbnail, stepped from Beetle Bailey's habitat toward her, upward, right off the page. She really didn't have time to see it clearly, but she caught her reflection in its yellowish eyes. "Yellow eyes on a cat?" was her immediate thought. She moved instinctively backward to avoid the oncoming cat and sloshed her tea down the front of her crisp white blouse. "Oh, hell," she muttered. Her supervisor, his tray in hand, eyed her with some curiosity. In the fifteen years Marie had worked at ValBank, he'd never heard anything stronger than a "Darn" from her lips.

"Something wrong, Marie?" he inquired. That was a strange look in her eyes.

"No, fine. I'm fine." Marie flushed as if she'd been caught reading a filthy novel, the kind some of the girls kept in their desks. She looked closely at the cartoon strip; nothing remotely resembling a cat anywhere on the page. Not even a Garfield. "I know I saw it--saw something," she said aloud.

Back at her desk, Marie went online and read everything she could find about black cats. She scoffed at it all: superstition, silliness, bad luck, evil omens, companion to witches. Her neatly clipped fingernails whiffed away the information from the screen almost as quickly as her manicured mind discounted it. Her life was as orderly and outlined as a first-year teacher's lesson plans. She intended to keep it that way. Black cats just didn't figure in. Still, she kept her mind on alert the rest of the day and into the next. She didn't intend to be taken by surprise again. Lord knows what she might do or say at the next appearance. By the end of the next workday, facing the weekend and leaving her desk neatly arranged, Marie had almost decided she'd been mistaken about the cat. When she left the office she wasn't thinking about it at all.

Marie was turning into her driveway when the black cat skittered across the asphalt. "Damn!" She slammed her foot on the brake, and the car bucked and died. Marie thought shakily, "I could have killed it!"

Then she looked again at the lawns on either side of the drive. No cat in sight. Uncanny. She couldn't have imagined that puffed up creature that looked anything but devilish as it dashed toward safety...or something. It hadn't been oozy or tiny; it was--this time--surely just a neighbor's cat. She had lived in her condo for almost ten years and old Mrs. Matthews' cat had been dead for at least half of those. Any tenants' cats were "inside" animals, and dogs were not allowed. That cat hadn't appeared frightened, hadn't looked as if it were fleeing neighborhood dogs. It had looked very domesticated, as if it had just heard its mistress calling and had hurried to make her happy. "I'm getting ridiculous," Marie thought, "giving not only credence to this cat but also personality." Sheer coincidence that a lost cat had crossed her driveway at precisely the moment she drove in.

Marie, however, continued to look for the cat as she parked. She perfectly lined up the car in her driveway with just enough space to prevent her getting her shoes damp as she stepped out. No, it was a real cat this time. She wasn't going off the deep end. As she routinely changed into neat slacks and sweater and then prepared her properly thought-out dinner, she was also thinking: her mother was fine, no problem there; her job was fine, a promotion soon and thoroughly deserved; her friends were okay, there if she needed them. She hadn't seen any movies or read any books dealing with the occult lately (not in years, she just didn't see the point), she hadn't taken any new medication (or any medication except an occasional aspirin; she didn't intend to end up on Valium or some such aid to living). No, everything was perfectly all right in her life. Just to be sure, she picked up the phone.

"Mother, it's Marie. Are you okay?"

"Fine. Al Sammons is visiting, from over on Oakdown. Remember him?"

Marie didn't want to know about her mother's gentleman caller, but she continued the conversation for a few moments. Her mother finally asked, "What's bothering you, Marie. You're saying all the right things, but there's something not right. Have you lost your job? All this NAFTA stuff."

"I'm sure to get my promotion, Mother. But, there is something..." Marie didn't know what she wanted to know. "Did we ever have cats...I mean, before I was old enough to remember?"

"Never. Charles was allergic. Are you getting a cat?"

Marie almost confessed that she wasn't exactly getting a cat, but a cat was getting to her. What was wrong with her? She hung up as quickly as possible.

Old Mr. Sammons still calling on her mother. Her mother, at seventy-five and nearly bedfast, still entertaining male friends. Marie proceeded to clear the table while trying to clear her head. She had her world under control. At least, she had--until the cat intruded. What was it all about? Well, it might be nice to have a cat to cuddle and hold, something to warm her lap, something to talk to. But black cats?

So Marie wasn't unprepared for the cat in the television set. This one projected a fierceness, a determination, an aggressiveness lacking in the other "visitors."

And the cat was coming closer: interstate, work, driveway, bedroom. Closer. And more and more alive. The driveway cat had seemed very real. The one on television stayed longer and ballooned outward toward the Marie. Rather than flinching or resisting its presence, Marie felt something in her issuing a welcome. The cat blacked out Marie's vision, and yet she was not afraid.

The doorbell shattered the moment. In a daze, Marie uncurled herself from the sofa. Jake, her two-doors-down neighbor, stood outside.

"Hey," he announced, a bit tentatively, "I know you're always busy, but damn, I'm lonesome. How about getting some cheese blintzes over at IHOP?"

Marie stretched and yawned daintily, showing a touch of pink tongue and a row of perfect white teeth. She tilted her head to one side, sleeked her hair back, and nodded. "Okay."

She knew Jake had expected the usual no or an elaborate excuse. And she knew, as he followed her to his car, that he surely admired the feline grace of her walk. She expected he would grow to like the new expression in her eyes and their yellowish glint.

Dingy

The eyeball splatted against the car window on the left hand passenger side and was gone, leaving, if anything, a slight smear. But Baby Bliss had seen it. She was sure of it and she promptly bent over and threw up gobbets of a Snicker bar and orange soda pop. Mostly the mess landed on the shoes of her older sister Muriel and the floor of the two-toned Oldsmobile. Muriel yanked Baby Bliss backward onto the seat; tears mixed with some froth at her mouth.

"It was a eyeball," Baby Bliss cried. "Didn't you see it? It was a black eyeball!" She wiped her mouth with her sleeve and Muriel pulled her own sweater up to dry her tears. Baby Bliss was three years going on four and her observations were generally to be trusted. Her sharp eyes could detect a glint in the darkness of the trees in their yard, a penny on the sidewalk, a kitten skittering away. "Maybe it was blue," she said. "It might have been blue."

"Nah, you didn't see no eyeball," Pretty Girl said. She had been looking out the other window, occasionally drawing her face back to admire her reflected features. Her feet were tucked up in the back seat to avoid the dead dog on the floor. Muriel, seated in the middle had slanted her feet to the left and thus directly under Baby Bliss's upheaval.

"Yuk and gunk. It's enough to make me sick," Muriel said. She looked around for something to clean her new shoes with but saw only the blanket on the dog. She slipped the sneakers off and, careful not to touch Dingy's stiff head, wiped them on the back of the front seat. Not one bit of vomit had touched her sister's black patent shoes that Grandma had bought her last month at Shoe Carnival.

"Did see it, too. I bet it was a sign," Baby Bliss said. She repeated her grandmother's words every time something unexplainable happened, "It's a sign. Mark my words, it's a sign."

Muriel looked back at the highway. "I don't see nothing with a missing eyeball," she reported. A flash of memory or invention flickered across her eyes: a slight hump a few moments ago, maybe something at the edge of the road. Baby Bliss had screwed up her eyes again, and her cute little cheeks (everybody said how cute she was) were getting redder. A squall was bound to happen, and Muriel couldn't stand her squalling, and she knew their daddy in the front seat would lose his patience. He'd already turned the radio up real loud to blot out any sounds from the back seat. "I don't want to hear a thing out of you three till we get there," he'd said as they'd returned to the car from the stop for gas and candy and soft drinks. "Not another word."

"I saw something back there," Muriel said quickly, looking straight at Baby Bliss who settled herself back in the seat, her legs straight out. "Guess the car just squished the eyes right out of something dead."

"Eyeball. One eye ball," Baby Bliss said. She was a stickler for literalness.

"Eyeball, then," Muriel agreed.

Of one accord the sisters glanced at Dingy, now dead almost three hours and going to his final resting place. His eyes were closed, but a tiny sliver of bluish tongue showed through his teeth.

The large vehicle rolled down the curves toward northern Alabama, its frame shaking when Joe Markum pushed it beyond fifty-five. Its balding tires barely passed North Carolina's inspection and wouldn't have if Joe hadn't known the owner of the station and hadn't sworn that he had to make the five-hour trip right now and he couldn't risk an expired sticker and had forgotten that little detail in all the recent troubles with his wife and children and now this dead dog on his hands and rebellion among the girls if Dingy wasn't returned to their former home for burial. Joe's friend shook his head in amazement at the recital and managed to overlook the tires. "Careful on the curves, Joe, or she'll take you off the edge," he had warned, slapping the sticker on the window.

Gotta get the kids away from here, were Joe's thoughts when he saw Dingy. His wife Sara sat on the porch and smiled. He'd seen that smile twice recently. Two weeks ago when their neighbor reported that something had poisoned his dog. And three days ago, when he'd found KitKat writhing behind the garage. Sara's smile was sad, its brilliance flashing; she had wonderfully white teeth and the bluest purest eyes...the eyes of a china doll. He'd turned her shoulders toward him when KitKat had jerked one last time and tried to see something in those eyes. She'd smiled and said, "I'll fix supper now."

"Did you...did you feed KitKat something?" Joe hadn't liked the gray cat, had resented its adopting his girls, had insisted it stay outside. But he didn't like seeing it dead either. Sara set a pan on the stove and Joe pulled a plastic bag from under the sink. He took the cat a few streets over and threw it into one of the dumpsters behind Burger King. The girls would wonder and cry and ask about KitKat. Joe would pretend ignorance. He figured Sara would too.

"Mama's just staring into space," Muriel reported. That was two days ago.

"She's not talking at all," Pretty Girl added. The girls didn't know what to make of their mama, now that she'd come home after all those months when Grandma stayed with them.

"Mama's smiling." Baby Bliss tugged at her father's pants leg.

"Maybe your mama's happy," Joe said.

"I said Mama's smiling," the baby repeated. She had her mother's blue eyes but Joe felt he could melt into them, not slide off the icy edge. A three-year-old should want to

57

climb on her mama's sweet knee, should lean against her thigh for comfort. Thumb tucked into her ear, Baby Bliss stood back and watched. Sara looked far over her head and had not yet tried to pick her up.

"Where's Pretty Girl?" Joe asked. He knew he was getting paranoid; he wanted to keep all the girls within view but that was impossible. He didn't get home until after they fluttered in from the school bus. He hurried home every day with a knotted stomach; he ate Rolaids by the dozen.

Pretty Girl slipped the golden chain into her pocket and slipped out of her parents' bedroom. Now that she knew they were going to Alabama she didn't fear getting caught and she wanted that necklace. Mama never wore it anyway. It had lain undisturbed on the royal blue velvet in the small white box for years, well, for as long as Pretty Girl could remember and she remembered the first time she'd seen it when she'd pushed a chair to the chest of drawers and stood on it to peek inside the small cedar chest box. The chain glittered in the tiny slit of light that almost seemed aimed at it, the curtains being drawn but the sunlight cut right across the box.

Since that day Pretty Girl had wanted the necklace. She checked on it whenever she could but that wasn't often. Being alone was a luxury in their family. She could reach the cedar jewelry box now without a chair, barely, and she was careful not to smear the thin layer of dust that coated the chest of drawers. If nobody wanted the necklace, Pretty Girl reckoned, if nobody ever wore it, then nobody would miss it. By nobody she meant her mother. She'd seen her mother looking at her oddly the last few days; maybe she was noticing how much they favored: how their blond hair had the same sheen and slight curl, how their noses were identical. Pretty Girl wished her ears were pierced; just about every girl she knew had holes in her ears, some had two in the same ear but Daddy wouldn't hear of it, and Mama wouldn't answer. Mama just stared at her or smiled. But if Pretty Girl smiled back, Mama's smile didn't broaden or lessen. One thing she didn't want was Mama's eyes, though they were just the prettiest blue. Pretty Girl practiced batting her eyelashes when she brushed her teeth and she gazed into her own greenish hazel eyes, thankful they weren't blue. People said it was a mystery that the three girls had different colored eyes: Muriel's were dark brown and Baby Bliss's were dark blue, kind of gauzy, soft. Pretty Girl closed the door quietly, took the blanket to Muriel, and went to sit on the front steps where she might wave daintily if someone came by and admired her.

Muriel looked at Dingy at her feet and tears welled to the breaking point on her lashes. Dingy was her dog really. One day he'd followed her home and Daddy had let them keep him. He was grown then and when he stretched out on the sofa, the girls could all touch some part of him as they waited for Daddy to come home. They established a routine with Dingy. He jumped up on the couch as soon as the girls settled down to watch TV and nibble Fig Newtons. His head lay in Muriel's lap and he rolled his eyes upward to see when a tiny bite might fall his way. Baby Bliss curled at his back feet; sometimes she examined his rough paws intently, smoothing the tufts of hair between the pads. Pretty Girl, having no room on the lumpy sofa, sat on the floor with her head near Dingy's back. If she thought he was getting too much attention from her sisters, she reached back and stroked his bristly fur. The girls were sure that Dingy watched TV with complete understanding, that his ears perked up and his eyes followed the sights on the TV. When dogs or cats were featured, they told him to pay attention, to look at that crazy dog or that silly cat. Now he was gone. Muriel felt very much alone, almost like a grown-up.

Grandma was old, all grandmas were, but Grandma Malisse wasn't real old. She wore her hair in a giant pile on her head and sprayed it to keep it there, and she wore purplish-brown eye shadow, even when she went walking up and down the two-lane paved road in her Easy Balance shoes. Grandma had a dozen pairs of little white socklets with red puff balls attached. Muriel thought they were so cute. Grandma's house was a two-story frame structure. It sat back from the road and to the left a field of little goats frolicked. She'd been left alone in the large house when her second husband, the girls called him JohnPaw, got hit by the mail carrier's car and died beside the mailbox. JohnPaw's children weren't happy that his new (of only ten years) wife inherited the house and a few acres so they didn't come visit her at all; Muriel was vastly curious about these hostile children, now doctors and school teachers in faraway states, who had (according to Grandma) hated the home place while they lived there and left the moment they could get to college.

Her daddy seemed awkward in Grandma's "new house," treading lightly as if one of the glass knickknacks would fall just because he was in the room. He always said they didn't have to eat in the dining room, the kitchen was good enough for them, but always Grandma set the table with her green and yellow Fiesta ware and glasses that tinkled when you flipped them with your fingernails. And the girls couldn't resist flipping them even when their daddy frowned slightly.

If Joe walked carefully in his mother's house, keeping his elbows tight against his body so that he wouldn't knock off a ceramic kitten or an angel, Muriel liked to wander through the rooms, touching the pretty pieces with care. She especially liked the angels scattered around; angels were her grandma's latest collecting craze. Their little faces peered from the mantle, from the end tables, from the shelves in the living room and the sinks in the bathrooms. Grandma was looking, she'd told Muriel, for a salt and pepper set of angels. Since then Muriel had hoped and almost prayed that she'd see such a set in some store and get her daddy to buy it. No luck so far. But Muriel bet that Grandma would find angels with holes in their heads or maybe in their wings. Grandma focused on her intentions.

One day when Grandma was staying with them,

Muriel had plopped down at the kitchen table. She sat a long time while Grandma poured blueberry muffin batter into the baking cups. Finally she asked, "Grandma, can I ask you a question?" The beehive head bobbed as she stooped to open the oven door. "Can you make something happen by thinking about it?" No answer. "I mean, like, if I wanted a boy to notice me or something?" Not that Muriel wanted any boy to notice her. Grandma began to rinse the utensils and mixing bowl. "I mean if you wanted something to happen real bad?"

Maybe Grandma misheard the question since the water was running. She came over and sat down. "Bad? I don't know about that." She pushed a cuticle back on a softened hand. "But I know for a fact that when I wanted Lester to notice me...I know that I just focused real hard on him." Grandma's face was flushed from the baking and her makeup was damp. "I just focused," she repeated. Muriel looked down at the place mats. "I don't know for absolute sure what got his attention but I just focused hard and the next thing I knew he started coming around and that was that." Muriel stirred a few grains of salt around. "Grandma, could I come and live with you next summer?" she said. "When school's out?"

"Honey, you got to stay with your sisters," her grandma said. "Your daddy can't do it all." Sometimes Muriel got so tired of being the oldest sister. For a moment she wanted to bend over and lick the salt off the table, maybe make herself gag. She wanted to do something unexpected, to make Grandma notice her, notice the tiny scars under her ears, hardly visible, from her babyhood chicken pox, notice her neatly trimmed fingernails, or at least notice the new Timex watch she'd won for selling so many boxes of candy at school.

"Course," her grandma mused, "when Lester got hit, all my focusing didn't do a damn bit of good." Muriel's heart lifted. That's what she liked about Grandma; sometimes she'd come out with a curse word at the strangest times and she never ever apologized for them. Muriel carefully swept the salt into her hand and carried it to the sink. Maybe Grandma wouldn't answer now, but Muriel was sure she wouldn't forget her question. "I'll finish these dishes for you," she said.

Her grandmother wiped her face with a paper towel. "Bring me a cup of coffee, will you, Muriel?"

Maybe she'd get an answer this time. She had assumed more and more responsibility for Baby Bliss. Pretty Girl she couldn't boss around or even lead around. And now here was Dingy, dead. She glanced at the animal and froze her tears inside her eyelids. If she started crying, it'd set the baby off and that would upset Daddy. She hadn't told him what she'd seen, but then she wasn't sure of what she had seen. When she thought about telling Daddy, the words wouldn't come out of her mouth and a kind of mist clouded her mind. The more minutes and hours that intervened, the less she could penetrate that fog and be sure of what she'd seen or not seen. Mama sitting on the thin front porch, her feet curled under her, her toes showing dabs of red polish...the mist covering her. Mama toweling her hair in the sunlight...a glass sitting on the little wicker table close by her...the glass held a greenish liquid. Mama smiling and toweling her hair, glancing...Mama issuing the wheezing whistle through her front teeth to bring Dingy toward her...her mama's bare red toes and other feet near the porch...where did they come from... whose were they...Dingy padding around the side of the house, pausing beyond the front step...wheezing whistle...his claws making little whiffs in the dust...new white sneakers...Dingy responding, lightly bounding up the steps...steps...greenish water...bright sunlight on red toenails...white teeth, blue eyes...Dingy's head on Mama's lap...a half eaten sandwich on a yellow paper plate, olive-pepper lunch meat...dust. Muriel thought she was going crazy. She couldn't quite get the picture. The blurriness always crept in, fog on a bright day. She shook her head, desperately wanting to see clearly, yet when the fog thinned she became clammy, her upper lip misting as if she had just poked her face through a wet spider web.

It was one thing to expect your mother to come in an emergency and take care of your kids. It was another to expect her to want to keep them. Joe figured he'd face that bridge when he had to and that would be after burying Dingy. He thought he could smell the animal behind him but from the fussing going on, the girls didn't seem bothered. If only he'd gotten there first, he could have at least bagged the dog or something. When they saw him carrying the black plastic garbage bag, the girls set up such a renewed howl that he gave in. Baby Bliss hammered her fists on the floor and screamed. Muriel was the quietest. Tears ran down her face and dampened the neck of her T-shirt; she cried silently and held the dog for almost an hour. He'd finally carried the worn-out baby inside and deposited her in her bed. Pretty Girl seemed in shock, dazed. She'd stroked the dog's head with more tenderness than Joe thought she possessed.

As he stood dazed by their grief, Muriel had said with a firmness belying her puffy face, "We have to bury him somewhere safe. We have to take him to Grandma's."

Joe nodded; he already knew he had to go to Alabama. Sara sat in the porch swing, idly pushing back and forth, ignoring the screams, tears, bewilderment of the girls. Pretty Girl had slipped into the house, maybe to check on her baby sister. When Muriel called, "Bring a blanket from the closet," for once Pretty Girl obeyed without questioning. Joe wrapped the dog awkwardly in the blanket, while Muriel held its head. The blanket had been a wedding present from his mother.

In ten years the blanket had become thin, like his marriage, Joe thought. He flipped the radio to another station, gospel rock. He wouldn't trade his three girls for any amount of money, not even for a boy child, but he'd give his last cent if he could remember only the early months of marriage and not the rest, the times the blanket, thicker and warmer, had been pulled up to cover the sweaty-cooling couple. After each conception Sara strayed away mentally,

63

being pulled back from her silent world by the birth of another child. She drifted physically and emotionally; his neighbors told him of the first, the counselors at Sylvan Mental Health told him the second. He didn't see what he could do and so he did nothing except look after his kids and ignore Sara's eyes. And sign the papers after she'd poured the milk over the check out counter in the grocery store and then began slapping the amazed teenager at the cash register.

Joe shivered. When the time came, he hoped his girls would remember and tell the cops that after he'd thrown their belongings in the trunk of the car, after he'd laid the dead dog carefully on the floor, positioning its head on the hump, after he'd slammed the doors of the peeling Oldsmobile, he hoped they'd remember he had not gone back inside the house. He had intended to try to say goodbye to Sara. He saw her standing in the living room, a glass of greenish liquid to her lips. Yet she smiled, almost as if she were saying *Go on. There's nothing you can do here. Go on.* He recognized the smell. He recognized the smile. He'd turned and walked to the car. He had a dead dog to bury.

In the Shadow of Long Meg

The farm road split the large circle of stones right down the middle. Long Meg and maybe half (had Maggie counted them which she didn't, not being mathematical) her stone "daughters" on one side, the other stones arcing on the right side of the muddy ruts. After days of rain, mist, and insubstantial clouds, a stone circle in Cumbria had promised solidity, endurance, survival. Its name enticed Maggie: Meg, reminding her of her own Margaret shortened to Maggie, and daughters... the daughters she'd never had, the one daughter she had no more. Everything reminded her of mother-daughter relationships: clothing ads, articles in magazines, photos, this circle, these stones. Daughters were everywhere and her daughter was gone.

She'll never grow older intellectually. She may live for years, may outlive you, Margaret, but don't expect her mind to grow also. You must accept that.

You must accept. You must accept. That refrain had hammered behind her accepting eyes, had hammered behind her accepting voice. She had worked at acceptance. She thought she had conquered her fury; she thought she had crushed the whirling rages that had erupted often in the first years. At every milestone in her daughter's young life, Maggie's anger roiled, threatened--the first Christmas, the first uncoordinated step, the first of several special schools.

Her body will mature normally, or so we have every reason to expect. Sometimes that's hardest for a parent...she will look like other girls.

She had dealt with Jenny's growing, long-limbed body, and, in time, time and time again she patiently talked about the expected menses, unsure of how little her daughter understood; she had shown her the sanitary napkins, placed appropriately, as Jenny's eyes simply widened.

It's God's purpose. God has a plan. God has given you a beautiful daughter, beautiful, Margaret. You must accept what is.

She had quit going to church.

Maggie stepped from her small rental car into a dark puddle. Cumbria had been inundated with rain for days, five of which Maggie had endured, wrapped in a comforter in her Bed and Breakfast room, waiting for emotional ice to thaw, waiting for the sun to emerge. The late afternoon sunlight was uncertain, but she had dressed in a long sweater and found this circle. In her rain-bound days, she'd absorbed stacks of tourist literature, finished the novels purchased for flight time, exhausted her crossword puzzle books. She had ignored the romance novels the landlady brought her. The novels caused a new ripple of anger to stream through her. Their blurbs promising ultimate, everlasting love and sure-to-be-overcome obstacles were a betrayal of all she had experienced. She'd read with disgust:

> *Daphne, born to slavery, abducted by pirates, finds first savage desire and, after bouts of intense lovemaking masked as rape, true love in the arms of the handsome buccaneer who is in turn redeemed by such a prize and sails for king and country...*

Maggie had wanted to tear the pages from the book and eat them, regurgitate them. Stuttering something about making hot tea, the landlady had temporarily retreated. She returned, however, to apologize for the weather and to warn her lone guest not to drive in the frenzied storms...roads were clogged with abandoned vehicles, some bridges were out,

66

detours were the order of the day. Better to stay in and, and, read something.

Maggie shook her wet feet and slammed the rental car door hard enough to rock the small sedan. The air was damp, cool, unpleasant, stultifying. She breathed deeply, deep enough to make her diaphragm hurt; she exhaled and breathed again and again until the physical ache overwhelmed the other and she could walk without a sense of reeling. One time, thinking she was staggering on the sidewalk, Maggie had put out her hand to steady herself; her friend had assured her, "You're fine. You won't fall." Maggie didn't believe her. She learned to overcome the periphery swirling by deep breathing. The moon was a thin slice, a curved bow colored with a careful hand, a neat child's drawing of a sideway smiley mouth. A child's perception...

She's growing up, Maggie. Let her grow. Let her go. Yes, we've been through that...

The stones sat solid, unresisting, certain. Aiming beyond the rough circle toward "Long Meg," the single, taller, mother stone, Maggie stepped through the soggy grass, sinking until mud oozed over her walking shoes, with sucking sounds like a hungry child at her breast. Cows had pastured around Long Meg and Her Daughters. Maggie stepped into evidence of their being. Too late. She swiped her arm across her face to eradicate the pungent odor and barely paused to rake her shoe sideway against a thistle clump.

Three months ago, the telephone call. The police at the door. The identification, the funeral, the counselors, the friends whose words echoed endlessly like howls in a canyon, like waves shrieking, their sounds never stilled. Evidence indisputable, witnesses on the street. "She just ran out of the alley. No way could the driver stop in time." The limp body, already stiffening when she had to say "Yes, that's my baby, that's my daughter." What had Jenny been doing in the alley? How had she slipped away from her tutor-sitter that afternoon? Could a mother ever say why an alley dark, cluttered with garbage, appealed, why a child would stare from the eighth floor window so relentlessly at the space between avenue and boulevard. The straight and narrow space seemed to fascinate Jenny; she could see the worst of city life flowing there, not the big limos of the avenue, not the tourist stream of the boulevard, not the sedans and luxury cars which parked in the designated garage below their living quarters.

She's better off. Maggie saw or thought she saw that belief in their eyes. Then the next blow, the questions. Sexually active? No. She's a child. Yes. Evidence of intercourse, rough sex. Boys in the alley? Yes, the women joggers had seen two boys emerge from the alley as they had themselves hurried to the injured girl. Young-looking boys, no beards, slightly built. The boys had not looked at the girl as the traffic stalled and snarled around the accident. Caps hid their hair. Youngish, smallish, that's the best the joggers could recall; after all, they'd been more concerned with the girl, with helping a few others maintain a respectful distance while a nurse who happened on the scene attended to the girl and they waited for the ambulance.

"There's nothing we can do, Ma'am, without evidence of rape." The policeman didn't meet her eyes. "May have been consensual. We've talked to everybody whose name we have from the scene, but two boys...could be from anywhere. Yes, we'll check the tenants-- already have. No young kids in your building, youngest was your daughter. Couple of teenagers off in college." Day after day Maggie sat frozen, numb. She listened to policewomen, to churchmen, to friends who when they knew at least didn't say, "It's for the best, Maggie, she didn't suffer."

Maggie went once to visit the older couple who had seen her daughter dash from the alley, dash across in front of them and their terrier, slip between the cars. They'd heard the bump.

"I can't sleep," Maggie said, sipping apple cinnamon tea, allowing the terrier to nudge her ankles. "I keep seeing her, scared, running from those boys...I keep seeing her."

The woman glanced at her husband. "We've been out of town, dear. We haven't heard about any boys..."

The husband nodded. "She didn't look scared. She looked..." He searched his memory. "She looked, I'd say, happy...a terrible thing, to die so young..."

His voice trailed away and his wife said, "So gleeful. A beautiful girl. I could almost see her finishing a marathon or something, raising her arms in victory. Did she run, dear, for her school?" Maggie had told them nothing more. They need not know more than they had seen: a lovely girl dashing into the street, a lovely girl dead.

Then Maggie went to England.

The moon rose as Maggie watched, her feet soaked, her face alone in the light, the rest of her body in the shadow of Long Meg. She knew she didn't really hear a whisper but she heard the words.

And still the rains come
And still the moon shines
And still the cows shit
And still the grass grows.

The drizzle she felt on her face, the odor she breathed in, both rank and clean, the path back to her car oozed with mud, dotted with piles breaking, broken up at the edges, joining the earth, to be replenished by tomorrow's cows, as she would be replaced by tomorrow's seekers. Long Meg and Her Daughters would remain, split as they were by the straight narrow road.

On a Slant

Josh lived for three months on a slant.

"Dear kids," she wrote, *"You'd never believe your mother has to walk sideways just to stand up. My home is hotter than the top side of a sunning blacksnake, not that you've ever seen a blacksnake sunning, not on the sidewalks of Roanoke. Imagine the sun baking, imagine the heat in your father's eyes when he was blazing mad and tri-triple it, and you've got the temperature of my summer place."*

Josh, short for Jocelyn. God knows where her addle-headed mama came up with that name. Likely some true story magazine about a bad girl turned good or a good girl turned bad and mama would have known about both ends of that equation. Josh let the air whoosh by her as she swung the trailer door back and forth, fanning the inside, stirring the air before she could enter and prop the door open. The screen door, for which she was thankful, had two big rips in it but with careful tying with some kudzu vines, it kept most of the flying creatures out; those that made it inside died in the heat when she closed up her place for the morning and crept through the fields to work. So she lived with fried insects in the dying heat of the late afternoon.

"There's a spring close by," she wrote to a former neighbor, *"cool water's a blessing down here. And it's cool under the big sycamore trees, down under the bank a ways so the two cows don't bother it."*

They muddied the stream further down, standing in the water hoof-deep so that Josh wondered if they felt its effect at all, flicking their tails at the cousins of the dead flies in her living room, dipping their nostrils and wuffing in the shallows.

Josh stepped on the large rock she'd placed where a step had once been and heaved herself into the room, welcoming its shadows, stifling as they were. She swung her backpack to the floor where it slid toward the downward side of the trailer. Her toes in thin canvas shoes from the Dollar General gripped the floor as she leaned forward. After a few minutes, she could manage the slant pretty well. And she was grateful for it. Who was going to suspect someone was living in a trailer in the middle of a hot unplanted, former tomato patch in the middle of Sommer County in the off center of north Georgia.

"Nobody had lived here some time," she wrote her mother. *"That's why I got it so cheap."*

Dirt cheap, no rent at all. The trailer sat empty, hot, rusting, falling forward where foundation blocks had slipped. As far as Josh could tell, nobody claimed the trailer and she didn't want to know who owned the land. Some college graduate had probably inherited the family property and didn't ever intend to live there, maybe rent it out some day. Maybe the white house on the stone foundation two curves down the road was the old homestead. A "Rental property by RePro" sign stood in the front yard and a Suburban with Florida license plates sat in the driveway most mornings.

Josh squatted and with her left leg hooked the backpack and pulled it to her, retrieved a plastic bottle of water and took a long drink; it was wet and still cool. She rolled the bottle over her forehead and let the backpack begin its slide back to the base of the window. She stood and wedged the bottle on the counter, behind a loaf of white bread, limp but edible. Her shirt was soaked through, completely wet and she peeled herself out of it, hanging it neatly on a wire hanger that dangled from a cabinet drawer. Her bra followed. She studied it, ratty, yellowed, but a necessary item. She didn't quite dare to go to work without it, whether she considered it protection or provocation.

71

"*Mrs. Watson doesn't like me,*" she wrote to her former boss, "*but Mr. Watson's bound to keep me on. He knows a good worker when he sees one.*"

Mrs. Watson's eyes had shrewdly appraised the mature ripeness of her bosom, Josh was sure that was the term she used. And Mrs. Watson also knew she'd be a good worker. Better to have this one working around the place than risk some desperate seventeen-year-old looking for any summer work, more full of problems than strength or sense, not so filled out, but likely more tempting to a man's eye, even Watson's eye, and he'd been known to brush against women now and again, pretending innocence when they moved back, never thinking Mrs. Watson noticed, pulled her lips into a frown, and never offered those women "discounts" or freebies. With a nod, she'd given assent and left the room.

Mr. Watson shrugged and ground out his cigarette on the cement floor. He pushed the W-2 forms toward her.

"I won't be working enough for that," Josh said, "Just enough to get a ticket on to Idaho where my kids stay with my mother." The state of Idaho just slipped out and was apparently what she needed. Who would lie about wanting to get to Idaho?

"It's the regulation," Mr. Watson offered weakly, already thinking, Josh knew, that he could pay even less than minimum wage maybe.

"I don't need much," Josh helped him out. "I'm low maintenance this summer." She'd slept in the slanted trailer two nights and what she said was the truth.

Mr. Watson looked at this woman who was looking sideways at the display of honey. He didn't give a goddamn about her kids or her rent. He did need a steady worker through the tourist season.

"Five dollars a hour is about all I can afford," he said. "Can give you maybe twenty-five, thirty hours a week."

Josh ignored the government forms; he was hooked. And so far he hadn't done more than glance at her breasts. "What about some of this stuff?" She indicated the boxes, bins, bushel baskets of produce around them. He'd pulled down a heavy screen attachment to close out customers, it being close to seven o'clock. The open-faced building already smelled of peaches on the edge of rotten, tomatoes softening, cucumbers mushy.

Mr. Watson must have suddenly felt generous. "Take anything we can't sell in the morning," he said. "Save a little work that way."

Josh was glad she'd splurged on the two hotdogs for a dollar at the convenience store up the highway so her stomach wouldn't betray her. "Thanks," she said. "And five is fine, for now. What time in the morning?"

"Before eight, close to seven if you can make it." Mr. Watson didn't see a car, didn't know how she'd get here but that was her business. "Start by throwing out the rotten stuff, spray the rest, fill up the bins, set out what's been unloaded in the back." He grunted. "Both me and my wife's got bad backs. Need somebody to do the heavy lifting, now J.C.'s graduated and got a scholarship to West Point. West Point, by God. He's my cousin's boy." He pulled a packet from his pocket and offered her a Camel.

"No thanks," Josh said. "Never developed the habit." She didn't say her daddy'd died struggling for breath, with his forbidden cigarettes on the nightstand and her mother puffing away and wailing in the doorway. "I can take some of these peaches now," she said. "Peaches you don't get much out in Idaho." She hoped that was true, could tell by Mr. Watson's face that he didn't know and didn't care.

She'd thought what the absence of a car might imply to any employer. Watson's Fruit and Vegetable Stand was, in that regard, the perfect spot. A couple of hundred yards down the highway, a seedy one-story motel, The Blue Ridge, sat off on a side road, once the main highway. If she walked that way, anybody would think it was her destination since beyond was only a small dam and then National Forest land. This she knew from the talkative clerk at the convenience store. Once out of sight of Watson's misspelled Vegtable and Fruit Stand, she could cut across the field next to a boys' school and then walk the gravel road a mile or so. Rather than approach the trailer directly from the road, however, she slipped down a small incline and around an abandoned Christmas tree farm with its now tall, unkempt trees, alongside the dusty barbed wire fence overgrown with morning glories and blackberry briars and to her trailer slanted in the midst of the Joe Pye and Ironweed. A long walk and hot as hell but it might not be much worse than The Blue Ridge Motel--if only it had running water and a bath room.

"You wouldn't believe how pretty it is here," she wrote to her aunt. *"The mountains are in a haze every morning, not smog exactly, a real fog and they just rise up hazy and misty. The flowers are lovely, and the sunsets are orange and red. Not much traffic, you couldn't stand the peacefulness."*

The only noisy traffic was occasional squealing of tires as teenagers (she imagined) bet their lives rounding each curve, spraying gravel and throwing beer cans into the weeds, and the growling of shifting gears as dump trucks crept along the road, heavy as pregnant sows. One of these days a growling truck was bound to meet a speeding Mustang or a Dodge pickup in a blind curve. It happened apparently all over this part of Georgia, according to talk at the Fruit and Vegtable Stand. "Nother one of Jackson's boys wound up in the hospital last night. How his mama can stand it, I don't know. You'd think after his brother, them other boys would slow down, but no. He plowed right through a fence and was throwed out, lucky he didn't have a seatbelt on or he'd a-been killed when the car rolled over. All three of them's been sent to Atlanta with broke bones. The Jackson boy's the worse but he'll live they say."

The trailer, slanted like a tipsy box, its aluminum reinforcing edges gleaming in the moonlight, had looked to Josh like a refuge of the first order. She'd literally crawled to it on her hands and knees, dragging her backpack. One side of her face would show a bruise and her shoulder hurt.

"An acquaintance told me about this area," she wrote

to a friend, *"and was good enough to give me a ride."*

The trucker had left the main highway, his brooding face bulldoggish, after she'd refused to scoot closer to him, refused his roaming hand. She'd sensed danger when he yanked the semi- cab off onto the gravel road and asked bluntly, "What did ya think I picked you up for? Solitaire?" When he'd braked on a bad curve she'd scrambled to open the door. The bruises were the result of his grabbing and her tumbling to the kudzu covered ground. She'd rolled down the bank and was out of sight before he could stop the truck. He got out and stood looking, cursed a few times, turned to pee into the darkness and then slammed the door. Josh stayed out of sight until she heard the truck stop further on, turn around, and head back toward the highway. The trailer door opened easily and she'd slept on a slant as naturally as the cows flicked flies.

Josh stretched out on the floor. Her head on the shag carpet sent little puffs of dust upward. The grime of long years bit into her back but stretching felt good; she closed her eyes and let trickles of sweat soak into the waistband of her jeans. Considering she'd worn those jeans five days and walked and worked and sweated in them, they were amazingly clean. At every chance, she sponged off stains or smudges in the tiny toilet tucked behind the Fruit Stand. On payday she could surely get a ride down to Clayton and find a laundromat and another pair of pants at the Dollar General or a consignment shop. For long moments she kept her eyes closed until her head swirled away memory and she wasn't sure of whether she stood or lay or even existed.

"I am settling in very well here, like my job although it's more physical than when I worked at Blakemore," she wrote to former colleagues. *"I make enough to keep me in all the things I need and there's no real problems."*

She simply ignored the blisters on her feet caused by walking at least three miles in three-dollar shoes. She stopped by the convenience store's restroom to scrub all over and to wash her extra shirt which she then tucked into a plastic bag. She ate bananas, peaches, tomatoes, carrots, celery, cabbage, apples, pears--anything that didn't require cooking--and sandwiches made with peanut butter in the morning, before it almost melted to oil. Occasionally a customer at the Stand would say, "I'm going up to Joe's. Want me to bring you a cup of coffee on my way back?" She stayed far enough away from Mr. Watson so that his wife finally turned her back to them without wondering or peeping, and she never complained about the muck around back, the slippery backroom floor where she sorted, tossed, sprayed, unbagged and unboxed the fruits and vegetables. She'd thought the produce would be locally grown and some was but most was trucked in and unloaded at the back of the building, perhaps to preserve the illusion of homegrown even for the local customers.

If anybody cared about the "new woman working at Watsons" they did not seem particularly interested. It might have been different if she'd been younger but the graying streaks in her hair and her thickening hips meant the young neighborhood studs looked once but not twice. Her face was neither plump nor lean, her nose neither big nor stubby cute. A loose shirt obscured both her breasts and her hips. One boy had eyed her and described her shape in gestures to his buddies in the car; Mrs. Watson smiled to hear one of them mutter, "Might as well screw your aunt."

Josh's one particularity was the inability to look anyone directly in the eye. She looked to the side, to the other side, slightly to the left or right of ears...anywhere but directly at the person addressing her. Josh's askew glances Mrs. Watson noticed only on the second day of her work and she tried by increasing the volume of her voice and by placing her hands on her hips to steer Josh's eyes directly to hers. It didn't work.

The snake lay across the barely distinguishable path she'd made to the trailer. In the hot sunlight, flecks of brownish gold seemed to fly into the air, even as Josh stopped dead still and waited, her arms at her side, one holding her backpack, the other a brown paper bag with a cold drink and pimento cheese sandwich. She knew it wasn't a blacksnake; its pinkish body had brown bands running across it, with small dark splotches in between. Her chest was an instant dam, too thin to contain the pounding flood. Surely the thumping harshness would propel the snake along. She could see perhaps three feet before its tail diminished in the weeds. It was flattened out, its body not glistening but matte-like, with a wrinkle where it covered a small stick on the ground. A small white butterfly fluttered around the Queen Ann's Lace close to Josh's elbow; a cowbell sounded down by the stream, then a muted siren on the highway. Sweat dripped into her eyes but she couldn't lift her arms to wipe it away. Paralyzed, as before.

In the salty blur the snake expanded fuzzily. Oh God, Josh thought, I can't move. She didn't think she could step at all. To her left was its head, to step right where its tail disappeared into the high dusty weeds might be to encounter its mate. Josh stood, as before. Dampened by the cold bottle, the paper bag broke and the liter of Pepsi thumped at her feet. She jumped, and the snake slithered away faster than she wanted to believe possible, yet in slow motion before her sweaty eyes.

Josh picked up the Pepsi and hugged it to her side, its coolness assuring her of something, that she was alive, that an accident of picking up a used paper bag rather than plastic that day had broken the spell, that the snake was as vulnerable as she...assuring her of something.

Of course, if the snake, or any snake, had wanted the shelter, the security of the slanted trailer, it could have availed itself of dozens, hundreds of opportunities to enter, as Josh saw, cracks at doors, windows, floors. She had to believe no snake wanted where she lived.

"My place is lovely," she wrote to a friend, *"but too isolated to be a desirable location for tourists at any rate. I have peace and quiet galore."*

As she placed her backpack under her head later in the evening, soon after darkness enveloped the valley, she shuddered violently once, then closed her eyes, hoping for sleep. It came as always to her exhausted body and while other nights she had dreams of another life, this night her dreams slithered away, illusive as truth.

Josh awoke with an intense awareness of where she was, the light filtering through the dust motes, her white feet straight before her, her damp hair smelling slightly dank. The snake she was certain would make another appearance. For the next few days, she went about her routine as if she waited for something. Mr. Watson noticed and maneuvered his body closer, not touching. "Expecting a letter or something? Somebody coming to visit?" he asked.

She saw it, surely the same snake, by the stream, again stretched out, in no hurry, secure and lazing in the shadows. Had she not been alert, vigilant, she'd have missed it. It occupied a brownish log, had appropriated the very place Josh had thought to sit and soak her feet in the sluggish water. Its tongue flicked in and out as she watched. Intensely focused on the creature, she ran her own tongue over her dry lips. She'd looked up snakes in a paperback in the convenience store, and its markings told her copperhead. Her childhood knowledge told her poisonous; the book said "low toxicity." This time she carried no Pepsi to warn her and no stick to protect her, yet she stood, refusing to retreat. Not that she was sure she'd sit on the log if the snake did take itself off, but neither was she going to back up. Not yet, anyway. She looked down on the snake, sweating even while goose pimples prickled her arms. She stood so long that the cows on the other side of the stream went back to munching and then again raised their inquisitive heads to check on her presence. When she stood still they again resumed their chewing. Josh's eyes watched the snake's triangular head and long length, she and it poised for retreat or attack. The goose pimples calmed down on her arms and she became aware of a sharp stone biting into the toughened sole of her right foot. When the snake raised its head slightly Josh's eyes skewed away, and it gathered itself up, and took its leave with only a couple of final flicks. It veered not toward her but away, going home.

A softness came over Josh and she sank to the ground gracefully, assuming almost a true yoga position. Well, she thought, well... After a few seconds she glanced at the watching cows and giggled. "Silly cows," she said aloud. Then she slid her feet into the water, wincing at the ache it provided her raw blisters. Walking toward the trailer, she kept a close watch about her but she didn't expect to see the snake again. Not that day.

No one can remain unknown, even in rural north Georgia, and before the end of the summer a few people were aware of Josh's living quarters. Curious, Mr. Watson followed her one day and saw that The Blue Ridge was not her destination, saw her continue. And in the way of such places, piece by piece some people put together the puzzle. Mr. Watson didn't tell his wife, but one evening she referred to Josh as "burning up in that trailer on Aiken's property." Josh continued in ignorance of their knowledge, becoming friendly with local customers, joking with Sue at the convenience store, hitching a ride with Jim or Zack into town, returning to her metal box each evening.

"Living here is a challenge," she wrote to her former pastor, *"I am trying to face..."*

She decided to delay writing to the minister. She would wait.

It was mid-August when the snake reappeared. She'd been watching the ground, been watching logs and big rocks at the stream and on her route home. She didn't expect to see it almost at eye level. And she uttered a little "Yikes" under her breath. It curled atop a fence post at the outer limits of the Christmas tree farm, actually a post with a kind of platform on it, perhaps where the owner had once placed a martin or bluebird house. Josh stopped. She slipped the backpack from her shoulder to the ground. Waves of cold replaced waves of warmth on her arms, through her body. She steeled herself and stepped forward. She was maybe five feet from the creature. Everything in her wanted to step back, to stumble sideways, to leave it alone, to ignore what she saw. Instead she took another step toward it. One swift forward movement could bury its fangs in her bare arm, in her cheek, or neck. Its head pulled back on itself, aware, very aware, it watched her and flicked its tongue. She stood statue still. Took another step forward. She knew herself to be now at the most vulnerable posture. She had to stoop slightly to be eye level with the snake. Only three feet or so separated them. Josh raised her eyes, gray-blue, the gray-blue of early morning fog. With the inevitability of a rising fog and the imperceptibility of blanketed sunrise she brought her eyes directly level with those of the snake. They gazed at each other. Josh hoped her stone legs would not crumble, that she would not crash to the earth, not startle with any sudden movement. It was not now a question of retreat, not for Josh at any rate. The snake did not move, did not continue its flicking tongue action. She stared into those unblinking vertical pupils, memorizing her fear so it would always be a part of her, called forth by circumstance but not controlling. Josh took a step back carefully, soundlessly, then another step, all the while her eyes threaded straight with the snake's. When her foot snapped a twig, the copperhead shivered its body, uncoiled itself easily, descended the fencepost, found its way into the kudzu vines behind it.

"*Dear Mr. Trent,*" she wrote later that night, "*I will be returning to Roanoke in a few weeks when I finish my work here. I will testify against my husband. I will tell what I saw that day at the playground. I can face him and the town.*"

She extracted a slip of paper with the district attorney's address and copied it on the envelope. This letter she mailed.

"Looked straight at me," Mrs. Watson reported to her husband that next evening.

"Yep, me too," he replied. "And she's leaving at the end of the month."

A Coimbra State of Mind

She sat facing the dripping windows. Their fringed cloth shades half drawn meant she saw the lower two-thirds of the passing yellow and white buses, an occasional trolley, cars and trucks zipping or crawling depending on the traffic light at the bridge's intersection. Umbrellas were the uniform of the day except for the young men who sauntered in the drizzle, a few older men with bent heads (had the wife taken the family umbrella?), the laughing girls who tossed their long hair and dared the moisture to daunt them.

No sunshine this mid-morning; no sunshine for the past three mid-mornings but the hotel clerk remained optimistic, or perhaps his training had included never recognizing the possibility of daylong drenchings. The dampness suited her mood; the very slight breeze suited her inertia. A storm would have demanded some response; a heavy wind would have provoked some resistance; a bright sky might have required a parallel lifting of spirit. This morose sogginess without fury allowed her to simply sit and look: a dark-suited businessman darted between vehicles; two stooped elderly women hardly fit their shared umbrella between the front of one, the rear of the other bus as they limped across the halted stream of traffic. With complete confidence that the motorcyclist would stop, the brakes would hold on the cement truck, the taxi would swerve, that human beings would prevail over the wheeled tonnage, they proceeded in total fearlessness.

Dianna realized that her response to the movement in the street, albeit seen from a secure, warm hotel, was the first interest that had flickered across her consciousness in the four days she'd been in the Hotel Astoria in Portugal's premier university city, Coimbra.

Fifteen years ago, John had proposed in this hotel and fifteen years later and seven thousand miles away John told her what he now wanted-- another woman, prestige at a larger university where he would lecture on the finance of mega-agriculture, a family with the younger woman who would be in the new university circle "Mrs. Stewart" and not "the second Mrs. Stewart." Dianna didn't blame her for insisting that John leave the comfort of his department, his tennis club, his favored status among students for a position elsewhere. There Lisel would transform from the graduate student who broke up Dr. Stewart's marriage to the lovely, soon-surely-to-be-published poet and adoring wife.

Dianna had been backpacking through Europe, a gift to herself after finishing a degree in modern languages. She and Carlos, who had attached himself to her and whose Portugese helped acclimate her to the country, had stayed in Coimbra for almost three weeks; then, as most students, she saw the Astoria as staid, comfortable, too expensive for her beer budget. A few blocks away, her back against a lamp post, she'd been studying a map, trying to ignore re-living what she remembered of the night before, the motorcycle ride.

John had appeared in the Praca de Commerico. Stepping through the meandering pigeons, nodding to the woman roasting chestnuts, he had dropped to the green bench beside her, placed his knapsack between them, and begun their relationship with a simple "Hi" and a waft of clean lemon scent.

Four beers and four hours later they were in her *pensao*. That morning she'd rescued two calla lilies from the woman selling flowers near the square, and John's eyes went

82

immediately to the lilies displayed in the water glass in the bare room. They exchanged a few get-acquainted facts: he was from the Midwest, assisting a visiting professor from The University of Iowa here for a six-month term; a new doctorate with his resumes circulating without much hope of a full time job so soon; the credentials from one of the oldest universities in the world would look good and he was enjoying his stay, sharing a small apartment with two other guys who often brought girls in for the night, something Dianna could tell the fastidious John would not do. She told him during the first beer that she was currently traveling alone and that she was leaving in a few hours.

"I'm heading south, to the beaches on the Algarve before going on to Spain," she said. It wasn't his business that she'd only that morning rented the place.

"The South's awfully crowded this time of year. Stay on here and we can go to the Roman ruins at Conimbriga," John said.

"I'll be back," she told him. "Maybe then." Dianna liked his looks, the light stubble on his cheeks, that he had not succumbed to what she called "the graduate school beard." She liked his darker eyebrows over his light green eyes, his casual, rumpled khaki slacks which were scrupulously clean if unironed. She liked everything about him that she could see and later she liked all of him.

Dianna had been ready to fall in love, ready to marry. And when John joined her and they looked at the plain facade of Sao Tigio church, when they tossed pieces of bread to the pigeons, when they told each other just enough to ensure interest but nothing proclaiming long term alliance, when they touched beer-cooled fingers at the metal table outside the coffee shop, when they gazed across the Ponte Santa Clara at the convent turned army barracks, when he spoke politely to the waiter with none of the arrogance of some of the American men she had beers with, she felt a softening, a readiness to consider...depending, of course, on his love making.

Some weeks later, upon her return, that had proved

satisfactory. He was in those first days--and always, if she admitted it--not a particularly inventive lover but a confident one. In her three months in Europe Dianna had encountered several lovers, from college boys to local men, and she had learned much without sacrificing safety. She was determined not to return to Pennsylvania pregnant (which her older sisters had expected and her mother feared); so in the heat of removing clothes or not removing clothes, Dianna never lost that bit of dispassionate sanity that demanded a condom. Her pills she did not totally trust; after all, her younger sister Beth had been on the pill and she got pregnant not ten miles from home.

She had stayed on in Portugal, but not much in Coimbra. "I need my independence," she said. She liked the South, the beaches littered with dottery Brits, tea shops and innumerable dogs. She wandered through towns whose names she remembered only long enough to read the bus schedule, always returning to John and security. When after dinner at the domed Astoria with its art deco fixtures, its quiet dining room, its small bar proclaiming respectability, John had taken her hand and said, "Let's get married when I'm finished here," she had not hesitated. "Okay. But in Pennsylvania, okay?"

However, the wedding was not in her church, not the hometown affair that her sister, though three months pregnant, had enjoyed. When John unexpectedly received a short-term job in Texas, they flew home, were married in a courthouse before meeting her parents, and arrived on campus the night before John assumed the vacancy of an assistant professor.

Before the final revelation, Dianna had endured the pity of some faculty wives who suspected, had deflected the anger of others who perhaps saw in her loss the insecurity of their own marriages, the constant temptation of the clear skinned, eager-eyed, often predatory nature of the women in their husbands' classes. Of course, she'd been dignified, perhaps aided John's assumption of her "indifference." And, of course, he remained pleasant, sure that Dianna understood, even complacent in his belief that she was as ready as he to start fresh, to discard their life together as he discarded used coffee grounds each morning.

Dianna should have seen it coming: John liked freshness in all things. Their marriage was stale, orderly; their sex, routine. John changed his cologne each Christmas and July, choosing light, citrusy fragrances that were hardly noticed. John regularly replaced his scruffed briefcase and bought a new vehicle every two years. He wanted fresh fruit for breakfast and fresh flowers on the dinner table. He looked disgusted if a spotted banana or an overripe mango were left in the fruit bowl. He removed immediately the wilted rose, the browning lily.

I wove through the streets on the light Honda cycle owned by Peter who lived temporarily down the hall, lived there waiting for money from home, drunk most of the time, free with his possessions. "Take it," he slurred to me, "anytime you're brave enough...got a slick tire, one slicker than th'other." I'd picked up the key and in a few minutes was on the rainy street, my anger hardly dissipating as I bent over the bars. I was a novice at riding the bike, a novice at life I felt: dispossessed, unnecessary. First, a letter from Mother saying my room had been emptied, my things stored in the basement; undemanding, yet forever-taking Beth needed the larger space. With the letter in my hand, I opened the door to the apartment. In the tiny kitchen Carlos was nuzzling Lucinda, open faced, baby faced, sweet faced, Lucinda with her sweater pushed up, her hand on his butt. Since Carlos had shared my bed without sharing the rent, I expected a certain loyalty from him.

I crushed Mother's letter and its crinkling drew their attention. Carlos squinted at me, his glasses lay on the window sill. "Come here," he said. "There's enough of me for both of you." "My god, where did you pick up that line?" I said. "There's hardly enough of you for me." Lucinda pulled her sweater down and withdrew her hand, but they moved only a fraction from each other. I picked up a bottle almost empty but not quite and smashed it against the counter top; the wine splashed and the glass went everywhere. I held the neck of the bottle, jagged, in my hand, and I looked at it and at them. Carlos' eyes widened. I threw the balled-up letter and the bottle out the open window and left them staring at the broken glass on the floor.

I pushed the small bike hard, sliding on the occasional curve. The Avendia was straight for a long way as it paralleled the river; the wind on my face felt good. I was free, I was riding along the Mondego, I wasn't working in the family clothing store like baby Beth, hoping that the Lutheran minister's son would fall in love with me. Let Lucinda have Carlos. Let Beth have my room, let her have a baby. I had the night, the bike, the cool March air. I was free.

One moment the street was dark and empty, the next--too late--a thick figure in a long dark skirt, head covered by a loose black shawl detached from the shadows. The "thunk" as the back wheel of the bike hit her resounded, it seemed, long moments after I saw her flung against the heavy street lamp, and I jerked to correct the direction of the bike. There was only the "thunk" and the slight squeal of my tires--and the roar as I accelerated into the night. When the Avendia curved and left the river bank, when the street narrowed, I took one small street after another, knowing just enough about the city to return to the Praca de 8 Maio. My hands were sweating, I breathed unevenly, I gagged a little as I parked the bike down the steps where Peter kept a chain attached to the bars on the basement window. I locked the bike and sat on the damp steps before climbing the stairs. In my bed lay Carlos and Lucinda, sprawled as carelessly as old married people. I didn't brush my teeth. I took off my shoes and crawled in with them.

Dianna brushed her fine blond hair, touched up her lip gloss and was ready to welcome the dean and selected senior faculty members to John's annual backyard grilling. She hated it. She'd been too acquiescent when they first

86

married to disagree totally with John's style of entertaining, and through the years she had failed at changing his mind. Perversely, she thought, John himself knew that steaks on the grill, beer in the tub, Bermuda shorts on the guests simply didn't conform to the "image" of John and Dianna that his colleagues and students had. Her pleas, her stormy protests, her anger each spring went smoothly ignored by John. Dianna just knew these faculty members who laughed so heartily as they stood around the immaculate lawn, who knifed into the tender steaks with such enthusiasm, sniggered as they discussed the party.

John said, "They enjoy it, Honey. Most of them have to attend the coat and tie thing at the president's home next week. They like to drink beer and eat your potato salad." He patted her rear. "Never know what they're going to get in that potato salad!" It was her one small rebellion or innovation for the typical backyard party. Starting with their first party a few years after they'd bought the house, she'd made a potato salad unlike the typical Texas style and each year...eight or ten, she'd been creating a different potato salad for the party. Last year when she'd suspected his infidelity, she wanted to add arsenic or bits of glass, but she'd been content with snippets of marinated shrimp and a hint of port as the "secret" ingredients.

Sometimes she felt that her potato salads were the only creative aspect of her life, at least the only one John's friends celebrated. She worked in a major realty company's office, writing copy, making every piece of property sound enticing, charming, profitable, whatever. The realtors sometimes resented her copy; after all they had the job of making the property live up to her imagination, of selling the merits that Dianna invented from a quick pass-by look. Still the owners credited the company growth partly to Dianna's way with words. A colleague of John's said once: "Too bad you don't teach creative writing at the university! All those kids think they're gonna write the big novel and they're pale as death trying to get there." "Yeah, teach them how to write fairy tales, Dianna," chimed in another. "The miracle of the twenty-word masterpiece–selling the American dream," another said. Dianna demurely shook her head at the first comment, ignored the others, and said merely, "Let me get you another drink, Fred." She seethed as she smiled. She knew her ad copy lured buyers. Her stock in trade was not the dirt, the bricks, the basement, the property line; she dealt in the "might be" not the "had been," emphasizing not the past of the property but the possibility of the present. The house might be late 1800s, but buyers were early 2001 and wanted to think now and future.

"Dianna," a colleague chided her, "you're like a goose, waking up every morning in a new world." Was that a compliment or a criticism? True, she effectively blotted out the past beyond an occasional reference to last year's party or last week's dinner. If John alluded to their Portugal days, their meeting and courtship, she pulled the shades down in her eyes and mind.

The patio was "dressed" for the party. The lawn was immaculate. The grill was spotless and all the implements lay like tools at an operating table. Dianna's elegant linen pants and long shirt had just the right look of casual expense; she'd long since learned not to wear anything white and her outfits were invariably the envy of the women guests, even those who, it seemed to Dianna, deliberately flaunted any kind of dress code, the younger wives in jeans, the older women in flowing vibrant cottons with pounds of beads. Everything was ready for the assault of some twenty-seven hungry people. In spite of their yearly reminders, some would bring wine, cheese, specialty foods that must be placed somewhere, disturbing the order of the kitchen and dining nook. Knowing this, Dianna removed a large pottery dish from its usual spot and inserted it strategically into the pantry. The potato salad with its subtle hint of Roquefort, more than a hint of Tabasco sauce, and chopped oysters sat ready.

John chose the last fifteen minutes before the guests were due to remind her. "Tomorrow, Dianna, since you haven't done anything about it, I'm moving out." He held up a hand in appeasement or shield. "You've known this was coming. You know who she is. I've rented a ...."

"Is she coming tonight?" Dianna leaned against the counter, her hand close to a bottle of wine. The beautiful potato salad sat between them; she'd taken it from the refrigerator to show it to him.

John also eyed the salad, not quite trusting her to keep her hands on the counter, clenched and white as they were against the speckled gray marble. He tried a tentative smile, not answering her question. Dianna looked at her wedding ring and willed her fingers to relax.

"You know she's not." He shifted his weight slightly so his beginning paunch wasn't noticeable. "I'm telling you now so you can decide how to handle it, tell the people tonight or not. Up to you."

"The people," she noticed. Not friends, not buddies. If he thought of guests whom they entertained yearly, whom they saw occasionally at dinner parties, the club, the tennis courts, if they were "people" to him, they were even less to her.

His statement hadn't, of course, been news to her, but its timing had the power of a gasoline explosion: a whoosh that caught her unawares, unprepared, defenseless; a fiery all- consuming heat flowed through her and she'd held onto the counter with white knuckles while it seemed her very being, her life melted away before her. Outwardly beautiful steel in a $350 outfit, inwardly she oozed wax to her toenails. John had turned away, rearranged the perfectly aligned pepper mill and salt shaker. Dianna actually looked at her feet to be sure she was still solid rather than liquified by the surprised fury that burned so hot it paled her features.

The potato salad was a big success; everyone felt compelled to compliment this year's unusual combination of ingredients. Dianna, however, was sure she detected a certain fakiness in the bluster of George Alexander Shumont, he who always expected the use of both names. She heard a certain smirkiness in the drawling sweetness of Sue Langford, wife of the recently deposed chairman. By the time the last guest had left, she was exhausted from smiling and shrugging off the compliments, exhausted from deftly moving away from the casual way John touched her shoulder or back as they glided among the throng. John looked, to her irritation but not surprise, fresh and alert as he helped clean up. In silence she stacked the dishwasher while he wiped and put away the grill and tables. When at one o'clock he pulled his suitcases from the closet and began scooping shirts and underwear from the dresser drawers, she reclined, in silk pajamas, on their king-sized bed and watched, pleased to see that his energy had flagged and weariness stained his face. She knew the moment he realized she was scrutinizing him; he smoothed his face into a blandness and repeated what he'd said earlier.

"You've seen it coming, surely. I won't fight you unless you're unreasonable. After all," he reviewed a sock and, noting a thinness at the heel, tossed it and its mate into the wastebasket, "ours is a longer marriage than most these days. And no kids to consider." The bitterness was there, had been all these years at her choice to remain childless for reasons she did not express. Her sister Beth, meanwhile, had given their parents four grandchildren, each of which seemed perfection itself.

Rejected once more, her psyche screamed. *Not the favorite, not good enough.* Dianna smiled and John, as always, accepted the smile for what it appeared to be, not what it might have signaled. "I knew you'd understand," he said. He zipped the case closed with a satisfying sound.

"Stop packing, John," Dianna commanded. John jumped, so unexpected was the strength and determination in her voice. She swung her long legs over the side of the bed. "Put your suitcases away. Get mine out of the attic."

"Sweetheart..." John lined the cases against the wall.

"Do it, John. Just do it this minute."

I found the tiny capsule right where I'd kept it hidden all these years, in a pillbox behind my old hair blowers and curling iron. It had come to me by a strange route: an older woman in my childhood neighborhood with whom I often sat in my teenage years showed it to me one day. "What is it?" I'd asked. It looked like any medicine to me, maybe larger than most capsules. "Death," she said, her voice thin, wispy like her hair. She held it out to me. "Darling gave it to me, brought it back from the war. You know he was in intelligence." Aunt Faye, as I called her though we were unrelated, had lived next door to us all my life. Her black eyes were lively even as her body shriveled. For some reason she liked me and we spent a lot of time talking or just sitting. As she moved into her late 80s she talked more and more of "the end," assuring me she didn't fear so much the actual dying because she'd be with her "Darling," but she feared the pain she'd witnessed Darling suffer. "He intended to use this," she said, "but he couldn't remember where he'd hid it and I couldn't find it in time." I held the capsule in awe and whispered, "Death." "I intend to use it," she said. "But if I don't it's yours, Dianna. You understand these things." I didn't understand anything, but I nodded. I wasn't sure I believed in its powers. Maybe her Darling had been joking. She told me where she kept it and made me promise not to tell and to help her if ever she asked me to bring her the capsule. I nodded again. When I was called at college to come home to her funeral after she collapsed and died in church, I paid my respects to her elderly cousins and excused myself to find the capsule. I'd kept it since.

I went downstairs, while John snored contentedly, and took the potato salad from the refrigerator. Not much was left, perhaps a serving and a half. John never ate leftovers, but he didn't mind sharing with others. I visualized his movements: in the mid-afternoon he'd call Lisel to come over, reporting my absence, his satisfaction with the sudden change of plans; how much easier for him to finalize the sale of the house, leave his position, resign his club memberships, how much easier to explain that his wife'd left him, packed up and left. And when Lisel wanted to taste the famous potato salad, her girlfriend who'd been a guest already having reported its once-again success, when Lisel prepared a fruit plate for John, when she ladled the tasty salad onto her plate, and sat smiling at her beloved...

She had a few days in Coimbra, a few days at least since she'd flown first to London, maybe more before authorities came knocking or inquiries were made. In a day or so, she would make a discreet call to the university, pretend to want to sign up for one of John's classes. Then, perhaps she'd go south. Perhaps she could find a student who owned a motorcycle... she was not prepared to drive one herself, not in this horrendous traffic, not with her new hair style. But she'd like a ride down the Avendia, along the river.

Telling Mama

The deed was done.

Well, it would take a year in North Carolina–but the decision was made. One divorce coming up. Relief was my main emotion; the waffling, the do or don't had taken too long. Now my problem was telling my mother. I didn't want to blurt it out over Sunday dinner at her house, didn't want to take a chance and tell her before Sunday dinner. She might throw up her hands and make us pimento cheese sandwiches instead of fried chicken, potato salad, and banana pudding. I didn't want to tell her before her Thursday afternoon driving lesson; any distraction and she'd scare her instructor even more than usual. Friday was a bad day; she was getting a permanent then rather than her usual Wednesday appointment. She'd said, "I don't dare smell up Mr. Weston's car at my lesson." It would be cowardly to wait until after we'd stuffed ourselves at her table, soon-to-be ex-spouse and I, after our leisurely reclining on the porch for a couple of hours of gossip and burps, punctuated with swigs of iced tea.

My mother has a strong sense of honor. She'd think if I was going to divorce her favorite son-in-law, we certainly ought not to continue to sleep in the same house for a few weeks. No matter what she thought, she wouldn't ask if we were going to sleep in the same bed. She'd wonder if she should still call once a day and talk about her garden and the continuing household ailments to soon-to-be ex son-in-law. Could she still ask him to fix that broken window sash and carry those heavy bags of mulching material?

I was not the first in our family to do the deed. My mother's older sister had divorced in the early 1940s when it must have been a real shocker. But then, it was war time and she'd promptly joined the WAC and gone to serve her country, and returned with a new spouse. Our marriage, on the other hand, had survived a long two years past the first decade...and appeared to the family as stable, settled, secure. We didn't drink, fight, swear, run around, or do anything that called for action drastic as divorce. Our problem was not unhappiness exactly but the fatigue that came of concealing unhappiness. I should have acted miserable...that would have made it easier.

"Let's walk along the fence and I'll show you where the moles are digging up those bulbs you planted for us," I said. A slight breeze from the left caused me to change sides so my nostrils didn't close up from the smell of her permanent wave solution. John was refereeing a high school wrestling match somewhere. I'd picked up my mother at the beauty parlor, inviting her to dinner. I'd put the roast in the oven along with some water in the bottom of the pan and some onions for flavor.

"What's that smell?" she said, stopping to break off some dead iris tops.

"Your new perm?" I was getting my first sentence constructed in my head.

"No, that's not it. Do you like this strawberry-lemon lotion Marie used?"

"It's okay," I replied. We tramped along, stepping on the raised furrows made by some underground creature intent on destruction.

"What a mess," my mother said. "And not a thing you can do about it. Mary Jane has tried everything, traps, poison, newfangled gizmos from that garden shop, and her yard is just a maze. She's going to get Jamie to plow up the whole thing."

"Speaking of a mess," I said. I couldn't get too

interested really in destroying the mole population in a back yard that would next season be someone else's problem.

She smiled beatifically. "I've never had a mole anywhere near my yard."

"Mama," I said and watched her stamp her feet on the fresh dirt. She was going to have a time getting those Keds clean. She considered herself much more modern than her neighbor who still wore only black leather shoes, but she wasn't quite modern enough for socks. White Keds and nylon stockings for everyday activities Monday through Saturday; beige pumps for dress-up times and always on Sunday.

"We're getting a divorce," I said. "John and I are getting a divorce."

My mother stopped her stamping. The silence seemed so deep I could hear the moles underfoot scurrying for safety.

"Well, child," she said and that word brought tears to my eyes. "Well, I'll swear."

I looked over her head toward the house, willing the shine in my eyes to recede. Smoke was rolling through the open windows, through the back door.

"Yikes," I said.

"Lordy Mercy," she said. We ran toward the house and into the roiling smoke. I started for the telephone in the living room. She had more sense.

"I knew I smelled something," she declared, throwing open the oven door, clicking off the oven. We both started fanning the smoke with dishtowels and I cursed the silent smoke alarm. I'd known it didn't work. Its little red light had been out for weeks, but I'd ignored the signal.

"Throw it out," I yelled when she yanked the roast from the oven. Then common sense said, "Can we save it?" The odor of scorched onions and blackened beef actually made Mama's strawberry-lemon permanent wave smell delicious.

"Honey," my mother said as she kicked open the screen door and set the pan on the steps, "sometimes

95

something's burnt so bad it don't warrant saving."

We eyed the shriveled roast. "Don't even think it," she said. "You might think you can scrape it off and save it, but it's dried up inside."

"Let's get some sweet tea, Mama," I said, "and go sit on the front porch. I've got a lot to tell you."

Never Falter, Never Quail

At age sixty-six Faith became obsessed by her walk, or, to be blunt, by her ass walking. For the first time she could recall she actually said the word: ass. It was the walking in the mall with all the "old duffers" that did it—not uninhibit her language but cause her to wonder about her behind in action. As she and Eileen set their pace, briskly she thought, until other walkers passed them with a wave and a hello, Faith began to notice the swishing of hips, the swinging of buttocks, the way one person's butt hung low, another's high; the fit of pants and the tightness or looseness of fabric stretched and unstretched.

"Look at us," Eileen said, as they approached the huge mirrored side panels on the front of Dillards. "We look like two little ducks heading for shore." "Little" is not a word Faith would have applied to Eileen, size sixteen at least, and the reason they had started walking. One of the reasons. The main one, Faith admitted, was that Faith's doctor and his P.A. had pushed her to do something, now that Frank was gone.

"I don't need to lose weight," she said, her voice conveying a touch of insult.

"It's not about weight, Mrs. Station," the P.A. said. Faith liked the woman; she always called her Mrs. Station. The doctor, looking all of thirty-five (now that Faith had been his patient for some ten years), called her Faith and had since the first visit. Tempted as she was to call him Alex, she couldn't quite do it. Not yet anyway. But if she could say "ass," the next step would be "Alex."

Day after day she and Eileen rounded the corners and alcoves of the mall, hardly seeing the window displays, the occasional broken tiles, the changing of kiosks with the seasons. They became familiar with their frontal view as they neared three times each walking day the department store; they saw their profiles reflected in the plate glass of dozens of shops. But as Faith realized and finally said: "I've never seen my ass."

Eileen stumbled, caught off guard, halted in the middle of thinking of her grandchildren. That's all--Faith was sure--Eileen thought of; she wondered if they'd ever grow up and occupy some reasonable portion of Eileen's mind. Eileen surprised her. "Whoa! Say that again."

"I've never seen my behind, my butt, my..." Now Faith hesitated. She didn't want Eileen returning to their retirement village spreading the word—the word that Faith had flipped or something. "Never mind," she said, daunted by her very hesitation.

"What do you want to know about it?" Eileen refused to let the subject drop. "You've shopped enough, looked in those three-way mirrors surely."

Faith considered. "You can't walk too far in a department store, really walk."

"Walk in front of me," Eileen commanded. Faith increased her speed and her Comfort Strides squeaked minutely, like a scared mouse, as she turned the corner and headed toward "Adventure Land" with its darkness punctuated by gleaming neon machines forever squawking.

Eileen lumbered behind her, silent, observing, Faith assumed, her rear.

"Well, come on." Faith said. "How does it, how do I, how does it look?"

"It looks...ordinar...it looks normal to me." Eileen caught up with Faith. "It looks fine."

That bit of generality didn't help Faith one bit. She supposed it would take something really unusual to make a rear end look abnormal. But just how did "normal" look on a senior citizen in pale blue sweat pants and matching zip-up jacket? She and Eileen didn't have much to say to each other the rest of their walk. Faith sang under her breath. Eileen was probably in Oklahoma with her grandchildren, and Faith felt grumpy. She wanted more than normal, certainly more than ordinary. Even Eileen had paused, had not wanted to label her behind, her ass, as ordinary.

"Don't be such a worrywart," she said. "Who's going to see us? Who's going to care?" Faith carried a mirror she'd bought at Pier One. It was the lightest one they had but awkward to manage, nevertheless.

They had arrived at Dillard's door—much like a gray garage door except for the mirrored glass on either side. "Now, we just walk back the way we came and look into the mirror." Faith turned the mirror horizontally and Eileen took one side. "And we can see ourselves walking."

"It ought to work," Eileen grunted. "But I can't see well enough to tell. Maybe we're too far away." They had walked several feet, attempting to match their steps so the mirror didn't jiggle.

"Watch it, ladies," someone warned. They stopped abruptly as another walker strode by.

"Ouch," Faith said. Her corner of the mirror had slipped and landed, sharp, on her instep.

"Damn," muttered Eileen. "Tell me when you're going to put it down." She sucked her finger. "I've broken a nail, and I just had my manicure yesterday. Damn."

"Don't you starting cursing on me," Faith said. "I'm sorry. I'm not sure I can walk with this foot." While Eileen held the mirror, she bent to massage her injury, looking for evidence of blood, but finding none. She straightened up and groaned.

"I'm sorry, too, about the damn," Eileen said. "See what's happening to us all because of you and your..."

"I know. I know. Let's try again."

99

They hefted the mirror and held it first at eye level, which was too difficult. Then they lowered it to waist level, all the time looking straight ahead so they didn't walk into the grates surrounding the palm trees and glancing into the mirror, with Faith limping.

"We've gone too far. I can't tell a thing," Faith complained. "Let's back up, get closer to the big mirrors."

Apparently Eileen had no sense of balance when it came to walking backwards. In six steps, she crashed to the shiny tiled floor. The mirror slipped from their hands, spun a moment on one of its corners and then also hit the floor.

"It's only cracked," Faith told Eileen, who sat, stunned, for a moment. In no time, several other walkers came to their aid and, shooing Faith aside, pulled Eileen to her feet.

"Are you okay?" A woman brushed Eileen's back.

"Can we carry this somewhere for you?" A man held the mirror upright.

"Just put it over there, next to the trash can," Faith directed. "I'll ask the cleaning people to remove it before the mall opens."

"Before someone gets hurt." The man carried the mirror away. The other walkers moved on, assured that the two women had nothing broken, only their pride damaged.

"Do you think Pier One would give us a rebate?" Eileen had a frugal streak, even though Faith had paid for the mirror.

"That mirror was just too big for us," Faith said. "Forget it, and forget rebates. Anyway, you mean refunds."

They both hobbled to their car, to Eileen's car, not finishing their usual three circuits.

"Next time, we'll take hand mirrors," Faith said. "Watch out for that truck."

After Frank's death, Faith had stopped driving. She'd kept her license and her Buick Riviera, but she'd lost her nerve. She hadn't been with Frank the day he skidded on the black ice and ricocheted off the guardrail into the path of the

Hastings Furniture truck. Often, she wished she had been; perhaps her visions of the accident were more horrible than the reality. Her neighbors and nieces had prevented her from seeing the car or seeing Frank until he looked almost as he had the morning he ventured out—against her advice—to pick up a new fluorescent bulb for over the bathroom sink. Each time she drove she began to think of skidding, of the car going out of control. The steering wheel sometimes seemed to grow limp, melting under her hands, the car veering to the right or the left. Sometimes the pavement turned squishy and soft and she hurried to pull the car off such unsafe material. Once, only once, she crashed right into a mailbox, just inches from a child's tricycle in the yard. The nice young husband/father had driven her back to Meadowbrook Lane. Once inside, she found the bourbon Frank reserved for special occasions. Even when she wasn't driving, images of Frank's Toyota sliding in front of trucks haunted her—month after month. Her great niece took her to see a therapist—an hour wasted. All the woman did was listen, listen, listen. Realizing that she was, in fact, a road hazard, Faith decided on her own to give up driving for now. Gradually the visions dimmed as gradually her memory of Frank in his coffin dimmed, and she remembered him lanky and stooping, age spots on his face and hands, a receding hairline.

After long months, more than a year, Faith returned, her friends said, to "normal," but not to driving. Getting around became more and more a nuisance: friends, taxis, bridge buddies, churchwomen, and finally the local Geri-bus for the elderly. She moved to Hampton Hills Estates when she felt she was more trouble than she thought her friends thought she was worth. And she liked Hampton Hills. One of the movers parked her Buick in the neat garage. The wife of the maintenance man drove it occasionally, picking up something from the pharmacy or the grocery. She wanted to buy it, but Faith wasn't ready to give it up. Not yet.

In the residents' lounge, while Faith sipped her green tea and munched a fat-free graham cracker, she mused on her naiveté. If she'd grown up in a teacher-preacher household maybe that would account for it, but Faith's father ran a machine in the Mead Paper Mill and her mother didn't work outside the household. She was sure she'd never even heard the word *ass* or any other anatomical terms until high school, and then only the most vulgar boys said, "Kiss my a...." College was a Methodist institution and employment thereafter was, first, director of Christian Education and then kindergarten teacher; neither environment offered great opportunity for straight talk. Then marriage to a good man. The minister had stressed Frank's purity of mind, his clean living. She was living proof that her generation was different from those that followed. Should that make her feel better? Would she die defeated in her simple quest? For a moment she indulged in sheer imagining: Faith laid out in her coffin, silver lining, prim, proper, pearls in place, fingernails painted (she had pre-paid her cremation fees, all was arranged, but that didn't stop her visualizing...), hair—strawberry blond, with not a bluish tinge anywhere—perfectly in place.

"Hey, Faith." She turned to see Harold and two buddies bearing down on her. Why hadn't she stayed in her apartment, why had she carried her tea to the lounge where Harold apparently lived, so often was he there. His buddies could not keep up with Harold, so he made sure he spoke loudly enough for them to hear. "You going to join our talent show? Hey," he punched at her shoulder. "I hear you have a trick with mirrors! Haw. Haw. Haw."

Faith glared at him. If he'd been closer, she'd have been tempted to smack him, him and his Haw-Haw.

"Anytime you want some help, Miss Faith," Harold's sidekick, Maurice, said, "just you ask. You don't need to go endangering yourself, maybe break something." Maurice was at least ninety years old, tiny and bent, and so sweet natured that Faith wondered how he tolerated Harold's gruffness, or how Harold dealt with his eternal niceness. If

Harold extended his arm, Maurice would fit under it, so shrunken he'd become. And his soft voice was that of a nine-year-old.

"Thank you. And no thank you, Harold. No making a fool of myself show for me." Faith picked up her teacup, hoping they would move on.

"How's the foot?" Harold looked as if he actually cared. Where was that darn Eileen, Faith wondered? She was the one who lit up when Harold came around.

"I'm fine. Back to the mall in the morning," she said.

"You can't keep a good woman down," volunteered the other man, Richard, a recent addition to Hampton Hills. He must be desperate for friends, Faith thought, to be hanging around with Haw Haw. He didn't look desperate, though. Rather he looked as if he'd like to grin but wasn't sure he should. Shorter than Harold, taller than Maurice, rotund and balding, he looked nothing like Frank, but she noticed he had very good teeth, obviously his own, with a filling slightly darker giving away their authenticity.

"I'd like to give it a try. Haw Haw Haw."

"Excuse me, please. I'm meeting Eileen." She ate the final bit of cracker and started to rise. Richard extended a hand.

"Allow me," he said. His hand was firm, his nails trimmed, his palm dry.

She smiled at the three men who seemed now adrift and purposeless. "Thank you." Well aware that they followed her with their eyes as she left the lounge, she wondered, once again, just how she looked from behind. She gave a little twist, but her hip resisted and the twinge told her to quit being silly. She wasn't going to change the way she walked at this time of life.

"Quite a lady," Richard observed.

"First dibs," Maurice said. Then he giggled. "Just kidding, guys."

"Just what was she doing with a mirror in the mall?" Richard said. "Guess we'll never know."

"Can't get a thing out of Eileen," Harold admitted. "Her face just turns red."

Eileen was growing impatient the next morning. "This is not working, either," she announced. "We should have known if we couldn't see with that big mirror, these little things wouldn't do the trick."

"Our bifocals are just not adjusted right," Faith agreed.

"Trifocals for me, on top of cataract implants," Eileen said.

"Lens implants. They didn't put cataracts back in." Faith corrected Eileen every time she said she had cataract implants. She never changed.

"Whatever. Let's stop at the bagel place." The women had discovered that eating bagels required more effort than they wished to expend, but they bought strawberry cream cheese at Bag O'Bagels and moved down the food court to buy All-American chocolate chip cookies, on which they liberally spread the cream cheese.

"Ah, the best of both worlds," Eileen said. "And just why won't you participate in the talent show? You could sing that song you are forever singing and let us hear all the words. If you *know* all the words."

"And have Haw…Harold make some smart-ass comment about mirrors. He's determined to be the m.c., you know." Faith had waited, even practiced, and waited until the right moment to say "smart ass" and Eileen didn't even notice.

"Well, how many choices are there? Maurice couldn't be heard over the folding of napkins!" Her friend tongued the cream cheese from a cookie and dipped her plastic fork into the container for more.

"There's the new resident, Richard what's his name?"

"Richard West, and I did hear your not so well-chosen adjective." Eileen ignored the fork and swirled her finger in the cream cheese. "Harold has a fine voice for m-ceeing and he's funny, too."

"Well," Faith said. "He does have a voice that carries. And carries. And carries."

"Smart ass yourself." Eileen grinned. "I guess we've ruined our walking with these cookies. Might as well have another one. I'll buy this time." She pushed up from the table.

"Oatmeal raisin. No, make it peanut butter."

By the time they'd finished their mid-morning snack, Faith had another idea. "This is perfect," she said. "Video. I can get a video camera and you..."

"Mercy, you are obsessed. At least you're coming back to life," Eileen said; her expression showed she wished she hadn't added that last bit. "I'll do it, I'll do it. Just get the camera—and find a private place to do the 'shooting.'"

"I've been alive," Faith said, with a huff. "It's Frank who's dead."

Eileen didn't answer and soon they were skimming along in the lightweight Honda, Faith holding on and trying not to direct Eileen.

Yes, the activity director told her, there was a video camera available in the office. Was she going to capture the talent show on tape? She expected Faith would surely perform. For two hours, the young director, apparently born with a computer in one hand, a camera in the other, tried to train Faith in the intricate workings of the camera. "Sorry it's so heavy," she said more than once when Faith's arm drooped. "It's an older model. A new one isn't in the budget yet."

"To heck with it," Faith told Eileen. "Let's go to Best Buy."

With the help of a teenager named Jason, Faith purchased a small video camera, a "palmcorder," and within the hour had mastered it. The boy knew his craft and delighted in turning Faith into the owner and operator of a silver-gray camera, easy to hold, easy to focus. "I'm going to donate it to Hampton Hills," she told Jason, "as soon as my project is over."

"Got a talent show or something?" he asked.

"No," she said.

"Yes," Eileen said.

Jason chewed his gum and smiled. "I don't get a commission," he said, "but maybe if I sell enough I'll keep my job."

"If you lose it, you just come over to Hampton Hills," Eileen said. "We'll find a place for you; we always need helpers."

"The talent show's on the fourteenth," Faith said. "Bring your girlfriend and come laugh at us, with us."

"I just might do that," the boy said. "My grandmother expected to go there. But she died last winter."

"Faith is going to sing her special song," Eileen told him, grinning.

"Big mouth."

"The park is too cold this time of year," Eileen said. "And the mall is not my idea of private—if you really are going through with this."

"We can go over to the Assisted Living building around midnight," Faith said. "I have it on good authority that the nurse sleeps then. The halls will be deserted. We won't make any noise. Nobody will know."

Faith handed Eileen the camera, having repeated Jason's instructions several times. The hall was eerie, snores and whimpers emanated from behind closed doors; the faint scent of urine overlaid with Pine-Sol had settled like a thin river fog over the halls.

Faith pondered the fact that in the last few days her quest for a look at her ass had lessened, but she wasn't about to tell Eileen that. When she was determined, she was determined, even if what she had determined to know was trivial, meaningless, silly...all adjectives Eileen had injected into the conversation lately, along with why, why now?

"You know, in college, my first real boyfriend had a real cute behind. I used to stand at the dorm and watch him walk across campus," Faith said. "It was always more exciting to see him going than to see him approaching."

"You're weird, you know that?"

"I wonder—how did I, my ass, look to him. To anybody."

"God, an ass is an ass," Eileen was as close to anger as Faith had ever seen. Partly it was that she wanted to be in the lounge or wherever Haw Haw was rather than help Faith get through this determined phase. "And you're a donkey's ass!"

"Well, don't shout at me. I'll soon know and then I'll join the bridge brigade again. Okay, you stand at this end of the hall and I'll walk all the way down to the end. You may have to use the zoom. You remember how?"

"Just get going." Eileen held the camera to her eye. "This place gives me the creeps. And walk naturally, for goodness sake."

"I am, I'm trying." Yet Faith knew that her walk was not "natural." A sharp twinge told her she was overly pivoting her hips. She stopped, breathed deeply, and started again. Darn. She was rolling her buttocks more than she did "in real life." This was not working. She didn't want to look like a tramp, a trollop, a Daisy Mae or a Mae West prancing along. She just wanted to have on film a record of her natural walk...sexy or not, awkward or not, primly or not. She concentrated once more. Stopped and spoke to her feet, "Feet, act like you're strolling through the park."

She walked right into Richard.

"What in the hell are you doing here?" She didn't know which startled her more—Richard's body briefly engaged with hers or her own exclamation. "Hell" was another of those words she simply didn't admit to her spoken vocabulary. Yet here it sprang, explosive even, from her lips. From down the hall, she heard Eileen giggle; she must have seen Richard approaching and had not warned her, had *chosen* not to warn her. Meanwhile, here was Richard, grinning. A wilted yellow rose stuck from his shirt pocket.

"What are you doing in here—at this hour?" Faith drew back and spoke as commandingly as she could—in a stage whisper. She hoped they hadn't awakened the residents or the nurse. No, she could hear a faint snoring from the desk area.

"My sister is here. She called," he looked at his watch, "half an hour ago, couldn't sleep, wanted the latest copy of *Seventeen*. She loves that magazine. I'm always having to stop her from ordering mascara or teddies or something."

Eileen joined them, just as Faith said, "Oh."

Richard did not comment on the camera. The three stood in the hallway, awkward. Finally Faith said, "And don't ask!"

"Come on, ladies," Richard said. "We better get out of here." He lowered his voice even more. "The Hot Shot stays open all night. I'll treat if you're ready to—if you've finished our work here."

"I could eat a horse," Eileen said.

"When couldn't you?" Faith said, her stock response.

"Or, at least, cherry pie a la mode."

They tiptoed out of the building. Richard deposited the wilted rose on the desk in front of the head of the sleeping nurse.

The women had walked to the Assisted Living building, but Richard motioned toward the parking lot. Faith headed toward the cream colored Lincoln Town Car parked near the entrance.

"That's the nurse's car," Richard said. "Here's mine." He opened the doors of the purple PT Cruiser. Eileen and Faith exchanged glances. Apparently there was a lot they didn't know about this guy. A sister. A rose. A PT Cruiser.

At the Hot Shot, Eileen waved the camera and asked if she could video "the scene." She's certainly left her grandchildren somewhere, Faith thought.

"Sure," the waitress Mabel said. "Not much scene at this hour, just me."

"I just want to get the flavor of the place," Eileen said. She proceeded to walk around, shooting from first one angle then another, looking appraisingly at the counter with its tired pies and falling cakes, at the plastic booths, the old fashioned jukebox. The waitress pointed out that the jukebox had been there since the fifties, one of the few still operating in the state, maybe the country. Eileen zoomed in on its neon colors.

Faith sat primly, uncertain of herself in a way she had only a vague memory of feeling when she was maybe fifteen and went for the first and only time with a boy to a carnival.

"I've never been here," she said. "Interesting."

"Local color," Richard said. "Some of us come down occasionally—to load up on grease and salt, two ingredients our dining room is short on."

"We have very healthy food," Faith said. "But I'm having the German chocolate cake." Mabel didn't bother to jot down the order. "With two scoops of strawberry ice cream. And coffee. Regular."

Faith was proud of not yet having to order decaf coffee. So far, and she mentally knocked on wood each time she ordered "regular," she slept soundly, even after two cups. In case that changed, she intended to enjoy this small victory over her years.

"Too mundane," Eileen said of cherry pie and ordered the lemon meringue with chocolate ice cream in a dish.

Richard chose coconut cake with white filling. Faith was glad he didn't once allude to videoing. His tone as he described his sister's condition showed his dismay and his love. "She's the reason I moved to Hampton Hills. She's only going to get worse; in fact, she has regressed from *Elle* just a few weeks ago to *Mademoiselle*, and now to *Seventeen*." He stirred his decaf, having added two portions of half-and-half. "She was an editor for a publishing firm in Baltimore."

"Are you going to be in the talent show?" Eileen changed the subject, perhaps noticing the tears welling up in Faith's eyes. Faith tended to weep at the slightest story of grief or hurt.

"Yep. Believe it or not, I've been persuaded to play my one and only musical instrument. I'll let you buy my coffee if you guess what it is."

"Ha." For a moment, Faith could have sworn that Eileen's Ha sounded as if she'd been practicing with Haw Haw.

For a few minutes the two women guessed: trombone, flute, harp, finally even "the saw blade," something Faith had seen demonstrated on television. When Eileen looked at her watch and stifled a yawn, Richard said, "I play a mean harmonica."

"That was my very next guess," declared Faith.

"I enjoyed that," Eileen said when they were back at their apartments. "Good night, I mean, good morning."

Faith unlocked her friend's door and said, "Let's see what you got."

"Got? Oh, Lord, Faith, can't you forget your butt for a minute!"

Nevertheless, she followed Faith into the apartment and pulled the video camera from her canvas bag. While Faith drummed her fingers on the coffee table, Eileen fidgeted with various buttons and peered into the viewfinder.

"Darn," she said. "I must have erased it! All I've got is the Hot Shot. Not even my practice sessions. Not a thing here of you, Faith. Some good shots of that jukebox."

Faith threw up her hands in disgust. "Darn, and double darn. I'm going home."

The night of the talent show arrived, as Faith had dreaded it would. Having promised the activity director and Eileen, she was prepared to suffer through it, in a new pink silk dress. She would sing her song all the way through. Eileen had dared her, had, in fact, declared that she didn't think Faith knew more than the first two lines and she was "sick unto death" of those two.

After Harold's flamboyant introduction and his announcement that no one had heard her practice, Faith walked with all the confidence of a kindergarten teacher among her charges onto the stage, stood straight and untrembling, looked at the assembled jumble of an audience (there sat Jason and a girl), and sang: *Life is like a mountain railroad with an engineer that's brave. We must make the run successful from the cradle to the grave.* In the brief pause, she knew Eileen had her fingers crossed that she'd go on; in fact, Eileen had the darn video going. Faith smiled and continued, *Watch the curves, the fills, the tunnels; never falter, never quail. Keep your hand upon the throttle, and your eye upon the rail.*

Richard walked onto the stage, harmonica in hand. Surprised, Faith moved slightly to share the microphone with him. He accompanied her throughout the entire song, ending with the fourth verse: *As you roll across the trestle, spanning Jordan's swelling tide, you behold the Union Depot into which your train will glide; There you'll meet the Superintendent. God, the Father, God the Son, With the hearty joyous plaudit, "Weary pilgrim, welcome home."* Faith flung her arms wide, just as she'd once seen Carol Channing do. She felt good.

To the applause, she and Richard bowed theatrically, and Faith said, directly to Eileen, "Now you know why I sing only the first lines."

"I thought the words were "never fail," Richard whispered. "I like "never quail" better."

Faith and Richard were prevailed upon to sing and play "In the Good Old Summer Time" after the final act. And they were declared joint winners: free tickets and lunches at The Biltmore Estate.

"Quite a feat, Miss Nightingale," Maurice said. He had rushed backstage once the program was over.

"Nightingale was a nurse, not a singer," Harold said. He was admiring the video camera in Eileen's hands.

Richard's face had a sheen of perspiration which he wiped away with a handkerchief Faith handed him. Later as they walked from the activity room, he returned the handkerchief, letting his hand linger on Faith's. Then he dropped back a couple of steps.

"You do have a cute butt, Faith Station. Has anyone told you that lately?"

Faith blushed, glad he couldn't see her face. In her whole life, nobody had ever told her that. She hesitated and felt Richard's arm go around her waist, lightly. If not now, soon she would have to decide: did she want a man, a beau, she couldn't quite think "lover," did she want a companion who couldn't simply say the word "ass."

Spring Thaw

Anita's husband, obdurately silent on major issues of life or little issues of lipstick and pocket change, delighted in describing the chunks of phlegm he coughed up, its degree of yellow or red or striped, its thickness, consistency, and quantity. So on that February night at a Motel 6 under the looped ramp of Interstate 77, she left. It was no reasoned and rational undertaking or she wouldn't have picked up her overnight bag and walked away. In fact, it had all the shadings of plain stupidity: a cold night, a light snow brushing everything (if he realized that--this time--she was *really* gone, he could have followed her tracks), a town where they'd only stopped for coffee and gas refills on their trips back and forth between home and his relatives. It was impulse, pure and clear. Twenty years was long enough. Leave now or forever listen to graphic descriptions.

Howard was in the bathroom, would be there for a while. "I'm gone to the vending machine," Anita told him through the closed door. She hoisted the light bag, just weekend clothes and sleepwear, picked up her purse, and was out the door. The snow glistened in the glare of the parking lot lights, as clean and unsullied at this moment as it would be ever, she thought. Only a few people had pulled off the interstate to spend the night, most apparently preferring the slipping and sliding and pushing on. Her footprints were distinct for some minutes, then partially obscured by the snow. The cold snapped Anita's mind to the realization that she now had to go in some direction.

Two days later, though she didn't know it then, she woke up on the drafty side of a cabin, aware of cold seeping into her backside, aware too that the warmth from the stove on the other side of the room would keep her from freezing to death, if she stayed under the covers. She could hardly move under the weight of quilts and blankets piled high.

She shifted, grunted, pushed up on an elbow. Bundled up in plaids and brown, a figure across the room moved slightly, turned around and became a he. He looked at her and she looked at him, the fire crackled. He picked up a cup and poured hot water in it, lifted a jar from a shelf, tipped it to release honey into the cup and stirred. Anita had a dozen questions and didn't want to ask the most expected: where am I? Maybe he felt the same, not wanting to ask: who are you? She took the cup and quickly shifted it to hold its heat between blanketed hands. He squatted at the bedside and watched her.

The honey water tasted good; she drank greedily. Should she be afraid of this burly man of indeterminate age? His eyes were kind enough, quizzical under bushy brows. His lips were chapped at the edges; his beard could use a trim. Anita, who taught high school students domestic science and threw in a little etiquette along with recipes and advice, thought she should break the silence. "How did I get here?" Her voice was froggy, croaked, breaking.

He watched her still. Then he rose, brought back coffee for himself and a stool. "Found you long side the road, route 232." He drank. "Long way from anywhere--even here."

Anita didn't remember falling, just walking...out past the closed service station, out of sight of the interstate, swirling snow, past a few dim streetlights into darkness. She surely had some idea that a town lay ahead but she remembered ...just walking. The wind had picked up, snow fell faster; the brightness of the sky must have given her a sense of confidence. She kept off the pavement and her boots were soaked in a matter of minutes, but she didn't pay much attention. At one gray house she'd thought to stop but she kept walking. Her breathing was ragged, but something was smoothing out inside. Her battle became one with the elements. She intended to get somewhere. She remembered that thought: *I'll get somewhere.* Then she didn't think; she pushed her body to keep going. She had not once looked at her watch.

"Thank you." She drained the cup. "Thank you for rescuing me."

"From what?" he said.

"The mad snowman," Anita giggled. "I started hallucinating sometime along."

She saw her clothes spread out a few feet away, all of them. She had on a large cotton shirt.

Somehow she didn't feel embarrassed or frightened, just curious. "Why didn't you take me to the police station or somewhere like that?"

"I figured you didn't want the police station. It's not on that road." He drank coffee, then took both cups to the stove, filled them from the pot and returned. "I drink it black," he said.

"Okay." She sat straighter, noting that the cabin was small with a doorway indicating at least one other room. "I had a bag," she said vaguely.

"Didn't see one, wasn't near you," he said. "Call me Toby, by the way."

"Is that your name?"

"Close enough. Yours?"

"I'm...Marsha Ann," Anita said.

"Well, you're stuck here for now," he said. "Bigger snow than expected. I had a hard time bringing the jeep up the mountain."

"Where are we?"

"Does it matter?"

It didn't matter to Anita. She was warm enough--if not at her normal comfort level; she flexed her hands, wiggled her toes. No frostbite.

"You couldn't have been in the snow too long," he said. He stared into his cup. Finally he said, "I threw your bag as far into the woods as I could."

My clean socks, my underwear, my make up she thought. She had to grin. As if make up mattered at this point. She shrugged.

"I don't want to know who you are," Toby said.

"Fine by me."

"Figured anybody finds that bag'll go looking in Acker's woods, long way from here."

"I can't stay in this bed all day," Anita said. "Hand me my clothes."

He took another sip of coffee.

"Please."

He picked up the garments. "They're not real dry yet."

Anita put the empty cup on the floor, pulled the quilt over her head, and slept another four hours.

They settled into a routine that satisfied both of them. In snow that measured eighteen inches deep, Toby made trips to the woodpile and he tramped a trail to the outhouse. They sat for hours, saying little or nothing. Anita read the books scattered around, poetry (Rumi and Shelley), history (WWII and Mayan), and the novels of Trollope. Three days after her waking in the cabin, Toby had seemed restless, wandering, picking up and settling items. He opened the door to the adjoining room, the storage room he called it. When he was out of the cabin she'd been tempted to look in, to investigate but she hadn't.

He lugged a large frame into the room, placed it near the fire. "Got to get back to work," he said.

"What is that?"

"A loom. I weave." Toby carried more equipment out, began the task of threading the loom.

"Well," is all Anita could say.

He talked sporadically as he worked. "Dye my own yarn. This is from walnut," he said. "I've got two commissions to finish; they're promised before Easter."

"Commissions?" Anita watched his square hands treating the yarn delicately.

"Politician up in Washington. A senator, I think he said he was. Saw my work at the fair last fall."

Anita shouldered Toby aside one noon when he was stirring a pot of mixed beans soup. He resisted her nudge and tasted the soup. One of them had to move, and Toby stepped back. "I can cook, at least," Anita said. "You do all the outside work."

Sitting in front of the fireplace, she had given some thought to their roles, and her sense of fairness prevailed: she should certainly help with the chores, and cooking was a natural for her. The cabin shelves were winter-stocked with staples, cans, packages mixes. Soon they were eating dishes savory and interesting, given the limited supply of spices and ingredients. Scrambled eggs became quiches, cornbread became spoon bread, canned vegetables became tasty casseroles. Toby ate everything, it seemed, with equal relish, but his eyes crinkled when a fragrant chicken potpie was placed before him or a gingerbread mix came with a creamy sauce.

The snow took a long time in melting. Toby stayed at his loom most of the day, and sometimes Anita watched, marveling at his patience, his silent concentration as he worked. His behavior contrasted with the patterns he wove-- wild, jags and bursts of color, emotion warped and woven by a quiet, stolid man. Anita picked up and stared at the table runner he'd made for the politician. She couldn't see it fitting into what she visualized as a mahogany-filled dining room, chanderliered, elegant, Washington home. The strip of material danced with energy, almost shouted a fury, unleashed a rawness. It surely demanded rough pottery, sticks and stones and bones, the physical unconstrained rather than dainty china, thin crystal, silver sconces. She muttered these thoughts aloud as the piece trailed through her hands. She felt she ought to clench it to keep it motionless. Instead, she spread it over the cot.

"What?" Toby asked, his hands slowing, his eyes on the pattern--an emerging storm maybe, maybe sunset in gory reds streaming from grays, or sunrise to a saved sailor's eyes, or an unnamed frenzy of natural forces, lava, hot and rushing, flood, racing.

Anita voiced her question about the appropriateness of the table runner in, as she put it, "some smooth-talking senator's house."

Toby shrugged. "Who knows what's in his heart?"

"But on his table?"

"Don't try to imagine you know what goes where--or why," Toby said. He turned back to the loom, but Anita saw a haggardness in his eyes, eyes that usually reflected a calm spirit, or so she had thought.

"I hear this senator's been a P.O.W., seen the jungles of Vietnam, been lost in them." The yarn slipped from his fingers, just slightly tangled.

"I'm making some fresh coffee," Anita said, "to go with those scones from yesterday."

Toby swore under his breath as he smoothed the yarn, and nodded.

As the weeks wore on, they lost any initial shyness about their bodies. She saw Toby in his briefs, saw a military tattoo; he saw her braless and shirtless. Extreme modesty seemed irrelevant in the sexless environment. Anita occasionally dreamed of Toby coming to her bed but the dreams never included sex, simply anticipation. She wondered if among his snores and his occasional puppy dog "yelps" he dreamed of her. When she asked him to check a mole she could not see on her left shoulder blade, he did so without comment or reaction. "Looks okay" was his response. When she cut his long hair, when she could have caressed his neck and bare shoulders, she didn't think about it.

Toby wove steadily, his meticulous attention to the loom belying the flashing fury that flowed through the

118

material. Anita cooked and stared out the small kitchen window. She began writing in a spiral notebook, trying to make sense of her abrupt departure, her lack of anguish about abandoning Howard, her indifference to the gray strands that inevitably returned to her dark hair. She had covered twenty-five pages before she wrote *I lived prudently until a cough in a snowstorm...I have lived prudently long enough.* "That's it," she said out loud. "The first thing in all this fluff that speaks to me." Toby looked startled at her words, directed toward the fireplace and not toward him.

"Spring thaw's coming," Toby declared one morning. "I'm going down to mail the runner and wall hanging sometime this week." His unasked questions hung in the air like unattached pieces of thread in an otherwise complete piece. "I won't buy women's things in Stoner," he finally said. "I'll go over to the K-Mart outside Bluefield."

She didn't help him out, just made a list of groceries, her sizes in underpants and jeans, and toiletries they needed and watched him drive off two days later. But in his absence when she opened the cabin door, breathed deeply the crisp air, and shed two layers of clothes, a restlessness stirred. She watched the icicles dripping, making holes straight through the snow.

Toby brought back from town, along with a new jacket for her and supplies, a liter of Old Forester. He set it on the back of the table, and while he didn't open it or offer Anita a drink, he glanced at it fairly often. Anita noticed the first glances by accident but then she paid attention. Toby said he was going to finish the large wall hanging he'd been working on, "before the first crocus blooms."

"There's still snow on the ground," Anita said. A new dusting had, in fact, fallen during the night.

"You're from Tennessee, you know those little bastards pop through the snow." His voice roughened. "Little innocent creatures bound to die in the cold."

Anita started to say, "No, they don't," because she knew the first blooms didn't necessarily die. But she said nothing, merely shook her head to indicate she didn't agree.

His reference to Tennessee meant he'd looked in her purse, her driver's license, when he'd rescued her. He knew her name wasn't Marsha Anne. He'd called her that as easily as if it were the truth.

The bottle sat on the table, Toby continued to weave, but as Anita cooked, wrote in her journal, stared into the fireplace, she heard more muttered curses, more pauses for corrections, more pushing back of his chair in frustration than in the previous weeks. She noticed that Toby moved the Old Forester closer to his plate, his place at the table. She wondered, of course, she wondered, what Toby's "problem" was; she thought she didn't want to know; she thought she should be leaving...before he opened the bottle.

"I should be leaving," she said one morning. The sunlight was brilliant, glaring on the last of the snow. "Will you drive me into town, lend me fifty dollars, leave me at the bus station?" She carefully chose to tell him as they finished their pancakes, before Toby went to the loom.

"Tomorrow. Yes," Toby said. He reached for the bottle, cracked the seal and poured the liquid into his coffee cup. Anita looked at him, his eyes bloodshot in the early morning. She had heard no snores from his cot in several nights.

Throughout the day, Toby drank a shot or two at a time, mixing the bourbon with coffee, then with water, then with nothing. Grunting a refusal to lunch, he continued his weaving, cursing under his breath, once crashing his fist on the loom. When she set a mug of soup before him, she saw the bruise on his hand. It was late afternoon when he spoke.

"Best you move on now. You don't want to be around when I finish this bottle and the one in the jeep." His mouth was drawn, his eyes bleak, his voice very slightly slurry, but his hands, Anita noted, were steady. He looked like a man who desired comfort he would not accept.

"I can be ready in five minutes," she said, rising from the rocking chair. If she had left one man with his phlegm in a snowstorm, she could leave another with his demons in the springtime. A man for each season, she thought. A tentative smile touched her lips.

"I don't trust myself after awhile," Toby said. "They said I wasn't responsible, they said I could not have driven the car into that bridge on purpose, they blame chemicals, stress, the war. Me," he said, "Me, I blame me."

"You don't need to tell me anything, Toby. You won't see me again after today."

"Yeah. They said I should move on, maybe marry again, have another child, wipe my memory clean, forget it all." He looked straight at her. "You think you can do that? Do you?" His voice challenged; she could see he clenched his hands together.

"I don't know, Toby. In all this snow, safe here, I have thought so. Now, I will see for myself."

When he stood unsteadily, Anita said, "I'll drive."

Toby set his glass down. "Maybe you'll be like the old mariner, always moving on. Maybe I will move on too, but I'm stuck for now."

He fished keys from his jacket on the peg, tossed them on the table. "Let's go."

The sun was still shining, just barely. They'd be off the mountain before full dark. She'd get some coffee in him someplace down on the highway. Then she would take the first bus; she would get somewhere. She would leave him to his winter weaving, to his springtime grieving.

An Interlude in Leros

Lucy watched the mother dog, teats highly noticeable, no pups in sight, come from a street beyond, something rigid, not limply dead, held in her mouth. The yellowish beige dog nosed first in one clump of scrubby weeds, then another, turned, pranced confidently in one direction, then another, sniffed, decided, undecided, looked around as if wanting directions, then zoomed in on a clump looking no different from the others, perhaps a little larger. In she went, only her haunches showing, evidence of movement, undoubtedly digging, and then she turned neatly around and lifted her head and trotted to the three-foot high wall with its narrow, six-inch width, jumped up with the balance of a trapeze artist, trotted down its length, turned the corner, looked about to determine how to descend, checked out the trash container on the truck bed, turned again and again before jumping down to the outside walk. A spotted yellow-brown cat lay on the other end of the wall and watched impassively, even more so than Lucy.

Lucy unconsciously mimicked the Greek men she'd seen in the ferry lounges and outdoor tables who placed a packet of cigarettes in front of them as they drank and sat and smoked. She didn't particularly like the taste of the cigarettes she'd bought. She glanced at the animal again, took a pencil stub from her down vest pocket, and sketched its relaxed body, something about its casualness she envied. Tucking the drawing into the cigarette packet, she flicked her zippo lighter and thought, Here I am in Leros in a sunny clime, a holiday time, and I pass my time watching a little ugly dog deal with its life–as I ignore mine.

Damn, she thought, I'm beginning to think in rhyme. Not good. Three weeks before, Lucy had left her job as associate editor of a small and not growing magazine specializing in rhyming poetry for children. It had been, at best, a make-do job, one that fell easily into her lap once she and Barry met the Spillmans who had started the magazine.

Lucy allowed her thoughts to drift and she saw that once the dog had finished her task, she found a dusty and shady spot and curled up for a nap. That dog is focused, she thought.

Focus. That's what Barry constantly told her she lacked. Her ambition was not to become editor of Kids Wayz; not to become a poet herself, not to do anything. Caught up in the eddies and currents of her life at any given moment, she dealt with them, going with the flow. That meant the usual lunches with a few friends, the usual dinner parties three or four times a year ("Not too often," Barry announced, "or they'll think we're social climbers." "Which we are," she said, to be answered with a frown), the usual dining out, shopping, the usual 10 till 5 work at the office three or four days each week. Lucy was confident she could have done all the Kids Wayz work in much less time if only the Spellmans hadn't insisted on doing and undoing so much of the work for her. Still, the job demanded little effort; it was pleasant to be introduced as a magazine editor, less pleasing after the word "children" was pronounced. She learned to laugh and smile but after four years she wondered if her smiles and laughter made any difference. If she scowled at Barry's lawyer friends, would they recoil in horror? If she spoke bluntly about the silliness of her work, would her friends back off and wonder if they wanted to have lunch after all? Life, she decided, was simply too easy.

Once, she said that to her friend Rachel. Rachel's eyes darkened and her mouth pinched up a little. "Easy for you. You don't have any children."

If she'd said the same thing to another friend, she imagined Alecia saying, "Easy for you to say; you don't have a husband facing downsizing at age forty-seven." Lucy coughed, ground out the cigarette, and spent some moments imagining how each friend would react. Each one did, in fact, seem to have problems that they constantly chatted about, fretted about, fumed, or grew silent about: finances, unfaithful husbands, parents in ill health, children requiring the care of the young, teenagers requiring the strength of the gods, drugs, medications, even a sixteen-year-old's attempted suicide, a son in the army now of all times, sure to be sent to the desert somewhere. All their problems were real. Lucy didn't have them. No parents, no children, no financial woes, no health-threatening illnesses. Even her teeth were perfect. How could she add to their litany of woes by complaining about her quarterly teeth cleaning, the yearly mammogram? No, what she needed was a challenge. What she needed, Barry said, was focus. He didn't dare mention children. She'd put her miscarriages behind her, as she'd put the "cause"–an abortion at nineteen–behind her. Barry wouldn't adopt. At 8:37 at the most coveted table at Savoir Faire a month after her fortieth birthday, just after they had raised their champagne glasses to toast his own forty-fifth, he told her he'd be a father in a few months.

When the divorce was final, her friends expected her to be devastated. They were at an age where women were typically devastated...by loss of husband, security, money, coupled friends. Lucy dampened her exuberance for the most part, but alone she wandered aimlessly through the house. It was to be sold, profits split after three months, and Barry's lawyer told her she should be finding her own place. She strolled in bare feet on the plush carpet, she lay on the king-size bed with its pillows artfully arranged and stared at the ceiling, she lounged in the entertainment center...smiling all the time, whooping occasionally, shedding not one tear. She gazed thoughtfully at each painting on the walls before deciding she didn't want any of them. She didn't know what kind of art she wanted, but she didn't want the Thomas

Kincaide their best friends had not only given them but hung for them in the dining room; she could do without the sophisticated slashes of color–reds and yellows–in their bedroom although she'd picked them out and still liked them. One by one she discarded all the wall decorations and, as if released, swiftly, she paused in front of each piece of furniture and mentally marked it off. What did she want? Barry's measured tones assured her he'd be generous: they'd split the furniture, china, and general stuff, assuring her that she'd be "wise to choose something manageable," and further advising her that "money would be tight in her future" and she'd need what he allowed her to take. To hell with it all, she thought. Or to quote good King Lear, "oh reason not the need." She knew all that Barry said was true, she knew how some of her friends had fared with less accommodating divorcing husbands. What she resented was Barry's telling her to focus on what she would be doing, needing, going. So she'd told the travel agent to get her to some sunny islands. Not even a very original directive.

And now, here she was on the Dodacanese island of Leros watching a damn dog find its dusty spot, lie down, and wait. Content. All that I am not, Lucy thought.

The hotel owner's wife waddled through the room, picking her accustomed way through the innumerable tables, chairs, to hand Lucy a tourist brochure. "For you, you ask," Mrs. Santos said. "Boat to Kalymnous. At Xirocampos. Small boat."

"There isn't a ferry, then?" Lucy looked at the tattered brochure, its creases obliterating some words. A very small boat, it looked like, compared to the Dane line ferry she'd been on.

"A week." Mrs. Santos struggled. "Come a week."

"Okay, thanks a lot," Lucy said. She pushed upright and gestured toward a chair. "Won't you join me. Could we get some wine?"

The older woman's face lighted. "Wine, yes. I get." She expertly wound her way toward the bar, itself smothered by stacks of magazines, ashtrays, boxes, a broken television set, and dusty bottles. Chaos. Lucy had landed in a hotel in Lakki, the not-recommended town on Leros, a hotel not yet expecting the summer tourist trade (if it ever did), a hotel as casually run as she'd ever seen and no one at home would believe. She wanted to think that within a couple of weeks, the owners would throw out a third of the clutter, wipe the rest off, arrange it so guests could maneuver a path to the check in desk. It might be possible, but Mrs. Santos didn't seem concerned. She returned with two glasses of semi-cool wine and settled into the other chair. Lucy had emptied it of its pile of crumpled cardboard and old newspapers.

For the next hour the two women talked in the way two women can who do not know each other's language. They smiled and somehow Mrs. Santos learned that Lucy was (a shrug) traveling, not settled, not needed anywhere anytime soon. Lucy learned that the landlady (me Maria) had been married forty-three years, had one son who helped (a gesture) around the hotel but who preferred to ride his motorcycle (varoom, varoom) and to hang out with friends, smoking (Maria pantomimed lighting a cigarette, her shoulders slouching, her jaw slack). A daughter had four children, the light of their lives (wide smile), but lived miles away, perhaps over on the other side of the island. The glass of wine turned into two, then three glasses, accompanied by a loaf of bread from which they pulled chunks. Lucy declined the butter, noticing it was packaged exactly as in the U.S., and that Maria's plump fingers dallied patiently with the little tabs. Lucy looked at her own long manicured nails, her indulgence. She could have offered to open the packet, but instead they both grinned in triumph when Maria managed to break the barrier.

"This boat," Lucy said, "I would like to go." She'd been eying the brochure sporadically as they sat and talked.

"Tomorrow she go. I call taxi for you."

"Uh, okay." No dallying now, Lucy thought. "I want to return same day." If she stayed in the islands much longer, she'd be dropping all the articles in front of nouns. Amazing

126

how little they contributed, anyhow. Amazing how few words were needed.

The next morning Maria dispatched Lucy in a taxi with a rapid set of directions to the young driver to deliver his passenger to the larger of two boats docked at Xirocampos. "Safer. Bigger," she said. Lucy rubbed the sleep from her eyes and held on as the cab swerved through the almost deserted streets, expertly missing cats who dashed across the road, a couple of chickens who squawked indignantly, an old man who raised his fist in routine anger while he pulled the donkey to the side. Lucy wondered at her desire to take this early morning boat to the next island. Admittedly seeing the landscape before most people were stirring was a new experience; her days usually started after nine, not before seven.

Something surged in Lucy when the cab rounded a corner and thudded to a halt in front of the sea. Beyond the trees with their whitewashed bottoms, a boat bobbled at ease in the still water as someone moved about in the engine room. And her heart, her pulse, her stomach bobbed or burbled. It could have been that Lucy was simply not yet awake enough to fend off an emotional jolt; maybe, though, she had anticipated something of this sort. Otherwise, why was she even contemplating, no, going on this boat? A friend often translated her moods and behaviors into a complicity with the stars; maybe her Taurus had lined up perfectly with the moon and Pisces...whatever it would take to send an awareness of right now, right here through Lucy. She swung her legs from the cab, paid the boy, and followed him through the graveled parking area to the pier. He insisted on carrying her small day pack.

Two boats, she saw, were tied up at the cemented dock. The one on the left, smaller and scruffier, was presided over by an indifferent-looking unshaven man who, seeing them head toward the right, turned his back and bent to light a cigarette. Lucy recognized a certain fatalism in the slant of his shoulders. He knew he would get "the leftovers" and he was reconciled to his lot. Once the tourists arrived, there would be enough trade to keep him plying the waters. A man bulky in a down-filled vest stepped from the larger vessel and onto the pier. The cab driver transferred Lucy's knapsack to him, exchanged a barrage of words, cocked his head, and went over to greet the other man who still had his back turned to them.

"Jack." The man took her hand and guided her onto the boat. She felt awkward stepping from the solid cement to the shifting deck, and her hand tightened on his. "Careful," he said, jumping aboard. He placed her knapsack on a plastic bench that ran around the three sides of the boat.

"I'm Lucy." She didn't know if some boat protocol required her to introduce herself. He grunted a hello in Greek. In a few minutes while he placed a phone call, drank coffee, and adjusted various dials, a few other cars arrived plus three persons on foot. While they were hopping aboard, settling their possessions, deciding where to sit and talking vivaciously, Lucy looked around the boat. Well worn but well kept was her assessment. A couple of rips in the blue plastic seat coverings had been taped closed with thick gray tape. The bench had been wiped clean; the railings were unrusted, the floor swept. The smell of diesel fumes seemed to have a sweetness underneath.

The trip to Myrties, the small port on Kalymnous, took less than an hour, but it was an hour that changed Lucy's life. In a sense she was even aware of a transmutation; with the surging of the engine, the gliding through the sea, the muted conversations of the passengers, the reflection of a weak sun turning the water pink, she knew that somehow she connected. She'd expected a sleepy, just-get-me-there journey, but all her senses were on alert. She noted each crinkle and crevice in the rocks looming to the side of the boat; she heard each squish of the water against the boat, each change in the throttle of the engine, she understood Odysseus and every sailor who felt more at home, more certainty, in movement than on solid soil. She was at once exhilarated and immensely calm, throbbing with excitement and serenely settled, totally with the moment and

128

totally beyond it. Soaking in the brininess of the sea, entering the depths of the water, slicing into the light.

"Miss?" The word didn't register but the Styrofoam cup thrust toward her did. A waft of strong caffeine returned her to the cool touch of the railing, the chatter of other passengers. The young helper said, "Coffee." She automatically took the proffered cup and looked up. The boy gestured toward the cabin where the captain stood, his back to them. "He give."

"Oh, thank you. Thank ..uh, him." Lucy couldn't remember the captain's name. For a brief moment she resented the intrusion of this polite behavior. Did he send around refreshments to all the passengers? A quick glimpse over the rim of the cup revealed that she was alone in sipping coffee. Several men smoked. The family had given sodas to their children, a young woman had a baby nursing at her breast. The coffee was strong, stronger than any she'd had in these islands, and she had drunk some tar-like brew.

"You like?" The boy watched her with curiosity.

"Good. Good and strong," Lucy said. She had learned to master her taste buds rather than offend Maria. In fact, Greek coffee was growing on her. She sipped again and smiled and the boy turned to do something with a coil of rope. Looking beyond him, Lucy saw land, a great hulking pyramid of black rock, and to the left another island with a small pier jutting out.

"Telendos," the young mother said, her inflection and slightly raised voice indicating she was addressing Lucy. "Volcano," she said with pride. The other passengers suddenly seemed to have some degree of English and as the boat neared and then bounced against the dock, they and Lucy carried on an animated conversation in which the upheaval of Telendos was described, the population (small), the economy (tourists mostly, conveyed by gestures of sleeping heads and sipping drinks), the weather (stormy?). When they stepped onto the strip of cement and walked toward the taverna, they said goodbyes as if they'd been friends for years. To the several "enjoy your visit" and "coffee, Marcos" (pointing to the taverna), Lucy grinned and said "Goodbye. Greek." The captain's helper asked if she'd like a taxi called. "Later," she said. "I will have some breakfast here." The dog in front of the taverna door lazily moved, stretched, and sulked away at the shout of one of the men lounging nearby.

Almost seven years later, Lucy sat once more in the café, now much tidied up. No dogs dared linger outside; the tourists kept the new owners busy. Lucy sipped her coffee and told old Marcos who had sold his café but came each morning to drink espresso, "Tomorrow I go home." She looked at Jackie, six years old, perched on the counter, playing with the cat and the cash register. The young waiter helped him tap out amounts on the register. It was too early for most customers. "I want him to go to school in the states," she said. "He belongs there."

Marcos' seamed face tried for understanding. "Half Greek," he said. "Jack...Jack, can he let him go?"

"He says so. His wife, too. She has always known I'd leave."

Marcos swallowed his coffee and waved for more. "A long time," he said.

She knew he was remembering that morning when she sat and sat, through the breakfast hours, into lunch, watching the boat depart and return three times before she stood resolutely. "I will be back tomorrow," she'd said. Although Marcos then did not comprehend English nearly as well as now; she had talked to him as if he grasped each word, sensing that he understood more than words. "On boat?" and she'd replied, "On boat."

And each day for a week or more she came on the early boat, drank coffee, attuned herself to the sea. She went into Pothia occasionally, taking the bus, exploring the harbor streets; she went to Telendos once but found it too confining. She talked to Marcos each day, sometimes so rapidly that he merely nodded. One day she said, "I have now a job." Jack had asked her to deal with the tourists who spoke English and French (she brushed up, using an old textbook she found under the stacks of books in the hotel lobby). She made coffee, she polished the boat's fittings, she learned enough Greek to respond to the locals who took the boat. The boat made several runs daily, but she loved the early morning trip best. She stayed at the hotel and began to help Maria with small tasks. In the Mira Mar and on the boat, she felt content, easy with herself. She smiled easily, she laughed, she drank local wine and was amazed that the people simply accepted her. At some point she became Lucia. Undoubtedly they rolled their eyes, shrugged their shoulders, wondered about (as she thought they surely viewed her) "the crazy American."

Lucy and Jack became lovers within a month of her first boat trip. It seemed as inevitable as the rising of the sun and as natural. Probably anyone who wished to know could put a date to the first time they were alone. Jack dismissed the helper Alexis, and rather than tying up the boat, he turned it smoothly out to sea again. At some isolated inlet where no hut stood, no sign of life, he threw out the anchor, cut the engine, and stepped toward her. It was that simple. They shared a large whiskey from a bottle he produced and he spread a clean blanket on the floor. "Surprised?" he asked and she laughed and shook her head no. She had expected they would become lovers, but she'd waited for him to make the first move. It was lust and longing on her part, perhaps a need to assert that she was attractive to this compact, solid man. Later she accepted that she loved him but was not in love. He had watched her, appraised her, since that first day; they had sensed the tension, the awareness of each other. But he had not been crude or lewd; he offered her the pleasure of his body and she accepted. So their affair began and continued. They drank their whiskey each time; they laughed, they made love; they returned to the dock. Lucy was no fool; she knew Jack was married, the father of grown sons, a grandfather. If he wondered when she would leave Leros he did not ask. They seemed to talk very little: no

131

politics, no family stories, no nostalgia, no literature. She never prepared a meal for him or slept overnight by his side, yet she felt Jack knew her far better than Barry ever had.

Being a mistress and having Jack's child was not even as awkward as Lucy expected. Maria told her Jack's wife knew her condition, and his wife even came to visit her at the clinic. A large woman, seemingly sweet tempered and certain of her place in Jack's life, she said, "A beautiful boy." Maria had taught her the words. Her eyes were warm as they surveyed the baby, neutral when looking at Lucy. And through the next years, when the two met, though rarely, they spoke as distant cousins might. Lucy and Jack resumed their lovemaking and Jack came to visit their son every week.

She taught her child to call her lover Jack not Dad, but she told him, "He is your father."

"No, he can not live with us. We live with Maria. Aunt Maria."

Now Marcos asked, "And Maria, she know you leave?"

Lucy nodded. "I will bring Jackie back every summer. He will know the island." Her son waved to her. "It will be hard," she said. "But there comes a time..."

Marcos' eyes brimmed and he swallowed his coffee. "Jack is my friend," he said. "He hurts."

"He wants me to go, Marcos. It is time." She held his hand. "Remember when I told you...about Jackie?"

Marcos had beamed as if he were about to become a grandfather; he had hugged her. Then he turned somber, listening intently as Lucy said, "I will keep the baby. Maria will help. We can live at the hotel. Their son's apartment can be enlarged." and she had talked on and on. Later Maria told her that Marcos had said of Lucy that day, "Like a saint she was, her face all glowing."

"No saint, sure," Maria said.

Jack had grinned largely, even as she said, "Doctors told me I would never have a baby, could not get pregnant. I, I'm sorry..." Feeling supremely happy, she thought maybe she should feel sorry, sorry to be adding to Jack's responsibilities, worries. He patted her stomach. "Not sorry. Not me," he said. With a note of uncertainty he asked, "Whiskey? To celebrate?"

"Yes, yes. Today but no more." She was already showing, a roundness where a flatness had been. Jack, a father of five, could not have been totally surprised, observant as he was to all natural phenomena and shifts in the wind and his world.

In the months when she waited for the birth, attended by Maria, tolerated by Mr. Santos, Lucy often watched the dusty little dog. She had learned that its puppies had never been seen. Perhaps that first day its intense purposefulness had disguised loss and hurt. She could not know, but one day she began to sketch the animal as it nosed about...and the sketches grew. Words came to her and the "The Little Dog Who Nose" was created. Maria's grandchildren, hardly understanding the words, giggled at the drawings, and they named the dog "Tiago." Other sketches and stories followed with outrageous titles like "The Little Dog and Eye." Tiago's adventures took her from the shady hotel where she lived to the windmill in the waves at Aghina Marina, to the island of Patmos and up the Byzantium road to the hermit John's cave, to the back streets of Kalymnous, to the sponge-diving museum.

Later, with Jackie in his papoose carrier, Lucy always took her camera and her sketchbook. Ideas sprang from her head to her sketchbook as she imagined the little dog searching for an object (the lost umbrella of its owner), searching for a friend, and for its pups that were stolen. The sketches multiplied until when Jackie was two years old, she took them to Athens, and then to a Baltimore publisher willing to chance a semi-bilingual children's book with its mix of simple Greek and simple English and its gangly (one publisher said "ugly") little dog. Lucy found she must travel to the U.S. for consultations and publicity. Now the books were gaining in popularity. If she were available for increased marketing efforts, she was told, more money was assured. Sales were adequate enough for a major publisher to approach her, but she stayed loyal to the Baltimore firm who pushed just enough without demanding her life in return for her work.

Maria pampered Jackie and spoke only her language to him, insuring that he learned Greek along with English. He leaned over Lucy's shoulder as she drew the little dog, as she imagined Tiago rescuing everything lost.

When Jackie was five, the dog disappeared. They waited for her, they walked the length of the harbor to the ferry along the coast road. They inquired, they had flyers printed and posted them on all the utility poles. Finally Lucy and Jackie talked; she said they hoped Tiago had found a friend, had chosen to leave them, was living happily some miles away, would perhaps return. Jackie's dark, questioning eyes told her he didn't believe it for a minute. She crushed him to her breast. "Jackie, our doggie is gone. We can let her live in our hearts. Let's think of where she would be happiest and imagine her there." So began a new game for them: "I think Tiago is 'way over in Chora" and Jackie, his face sad, showing he knew they were kidding themselves, said "I think Tiago is in the butcher shop under Mr. Nick's feet."

They imagined Tiago in familiar and totally unfamiliar places, and when Jackie tired, he declared, "The doggie is in Never Never land." His tears came again and Lucy whispered, "Yes, there–and with us."

Tiago was never found. Mr. Santos said when it was their time, old dogs simply found a place and curled up to die. Lucy had seen that the animal was losing its hair, was walking with difficulty, and didn't seem to hear. From the "game" a new series emerged, as a little boy went searching for Doggie. The little boy was chubby, dark-haired, and lived with an immense family. Lucy populated his home with goats, chickens, a cow, bee hives...and the publisher wanted to publish before the following Christmas.

Jack and Lucy remained lovers through the years; she went with him on the boat, she made coffee, she designed brochures which he left in hotels on the islands. Both boats increased their business, and Mr. Unshaven (as Lucy privately called him) even smiled at her. One of Jack's sons added a third boat to the service. Paolo, the young taxi driver who, after that first morning, always drove Lucy to the boat became Jackie's godfather, adoring him, caring for him, installing a baby seat in his automobile at Lucy's insistence.

With each trip to the U.S. Lucy realized she was American at the core, that she wanted her son to grow up there. As she watched Jackie, dusty and barefoot, chase after Maria's old hen, she thought, Here I found my focus, something magical and now I must leave. This island was her Never Never land, a space, an interlude where she could flourish: a nurturing mother figure in Maria, love making with Jack, an artistic ability realized and recognized, admiring glances and flirtations with island men and tourists. And Jackie–her love and responsibility–was woven in a mantle she wore with pleasure. Her Leros life had been a balm, much needed, rich beyond her expectations. It showed her she could survive, open to new experiences. She could meet the demands of single parenthood as she edged toward fifty. In the mid-west, no boats would send surges through her senses, perhaps. But even Odysseus yearned for home and found his way there. And if he then turned seaward again, that option was also hers. Horizons weren't stable.

Now Lucy told Marcos, "I have a sister in Dayton, Ohio. She wants us to come there. She's sure I can get a job. Jackie will go to first grade."

The boat pulled into the harbor. Jack stood solid at the wheel. His hair had whitened around the ears; his eyebrows had become bushy. He jumped to the pier and started toward the café. Not knowing she watched, he stopped, put his hand over his heart for a moment, and came toward the building. Jackie jumped down and raced outside, "Jack, Jack, I can count. I know my numbers."

135

"Oh, my son," Jack swung him in the air. "I know my numbers too. I will miss you."

Lucy joined them, Marcos behind her. The sea sparkled, Telendos stood dark against the sky, diesel fumes permeated Jack's shirt. "I leave my heart behind," Lucy said to Jack. They were parting here; suitcases were piled inside the door.

"No, you take our heart with you." Jack hoisted Jackie onto his shoulders. They walked inside and had a final whiskey.

And the Animals Knelt

My grandmother had me on her lap and she smelled of fried chicken and freshly ironed apron. She held me because my mama just told me Daddy wouldn't be coming home for Christmas after all. He was in Manila or somewhere that made me think of vanilla when Mama's soft voice said it.

"Look at that pout," Grandma said, "and you such a pretty child when you smile."

I chewed on my pigtail. "I don't want to smile. I may never smile again."

"Now that's a big maybe. You best be careful of what you say tonight. Santa Claus might hear you–and it's about time for him to hitch his reindeer up and set out."

"Tommy said no old Santa's gonna find us back here in the mountains, anyway."

Grandma smoothed my hair with her rough hand. "I bet that Tommy will change his tune about midnight, specially if he hears little hooves a-pattering on the roof."

"He was awfully sure," I said. "I miss my Daddy." Daddy called me his brave little tomboy.

Grandma wasn't one for much talking. She shifted a little to get more comfortable. I always gave up Grandma's lap when little Gordie came toddling along. "After all," Mama said, "he's the baby, and he's never even seen his daddy yet . You're our big girl now."

"And old MaryBelle is sick," I said, piling on the misery. Daddy gone to war, Mama crying, little Gordie just too cute and cuddly, Santa likely to get lost, and now our cow, our only cow, had come down sick. "I think Christmas stinks!"

"Young lady, get off that pity pot of yours," Grandma said, her voice stern. "You go wash up the dishes for your mama and I'll tell you what we'll do at midnight."

"What?" I jumped off her lap in my excitement. "What will we do? I don't ever get to stay up till midnight. I never have. Will Mama let me?"

"Your mama's tired. She's in there crying right now because my Billy won't be home like he hoped and the army promised. We'll keep it our secret. Go on, now. Get those dishes done."

Grandma was rocking gently in front of the fireplace when I came back from the kitchen. I'd made so much noise Mama said from the bedroom, "Rachel Jean, if you wake this baby you're going to have to tend to him."

I pulled two cushions from the sofa—one to sit on and the other I held in my arms. It was silky and had fringe and a painting on it of white sand and palm trees. It was from that vanilla place where Daddy was soldiering. I sat down in front of the fire, careful not to block the heat from Grandma.

"My granddaddy told us this story," she began, "and I reckon it came over on the ships from England with his momma and poppa. Listen, child," and she cupped her hand to her ear.

I listened intently. I heard Mama scribbling on a piece of paper, writing Daddy again. Grandma leaned toward the window. The wind was blowing a strong snow, and the sashes crackled. I leaned toward the drafty window too and listened as hard as I could. A dog barked, old MaryBelle was lowing in the barn, her bell jangling a little, and Oscar the mule snorted. I thought I even heard the sow and her pigs eating at the trough. But I'd never heard all those sounds before...with the wind howling and the barn way off from the house.

"Granddaddy said on Christmas eve, the animals all stay awake till the dot of midnight," she whispered. "They're waiting to honor the Christ child. He was born in a manger, you know, like in the barn, born among strangers, not even a bed." Grandma's voice was so mournful I looked at her, expecting almost to see tears. But Grandma was tough. She never cried, and sometimes she got put out with Mama who cried a lot.

"The Sunday school teacher told us about little baby Jesus," I said, "and the preacher talked about his birthday." I thought a moment. "But they didn't say a word about animals, 'cept Joseph and Mary had a donkey."

Grandma had a faraway look in her eyes. "All the animals, they say, wait up for that blessed moment. Some people even say that right then they even talk to each other." She shook her head. "I don't know about that." She smiled and a little smile crept out to my lips. "Can you imagine what Oscar and MaryBelle would talk about? I bet your Daddy's fiesty fine mare wouldn't even speak to the rest of them, fancy as she is!"

Daddy had courted Mama on his shiny brown mare, Juliet, his pride and joy. Mama groomed her every week so when Daddy came home he wouldn't be ashamed of his horse.

I giggled a little but thinking of Juliet made me think of Daddy, and I hung my head again. "You don't believe that, do you, Grandma? Animals talking?"

"Christmas is a magic time, Rachel Jean, anything can happen. But," she admitted, "talking animals? More'n likely the other story's true." She paused so long I jiggled her shoe.

"What, Grandma, what?"

"All the animals in the world—with any sense, that is—kneel down at midnight to pay homage to the baby child Jesus. Yes, they do. Now that I can believe."

"Oh, Grandma, have you ever seen them do that, have you?" I had a vision of camels and elephants in far off places, and polar bears and black bears, and giraffes and billy goats all going down on their knees. It couldn't be.

139

"I admit, child, I've never stayed up to see," Grandma said. "With so much work to be done, I'm always asleep."

"We'll see tonight, Grandma, we'll stay up. Oh, I don't care if Tommy is right about Santa Claus. I don't think he'll get here tonight. Look, now it's snowing even harder."

"I've always wanted to see the animals on Christmas Eve," Grandma said, "but I never did. We'll go out there, no matter how cold." She bent over and stirred the fire. "Let's get some rest, child, first."

I tried and tried to rest but I was afraid I'd miss midnight. Truly I wasn't so sure about Santa Claus because I knew the army was bigger than Santa. I'd written and asked him to bring Daddy home, and then Mama got his letter and had been crying ever since.

I woke up Grandma who was snoring loud enough to keep any reindeer off the roof. She rubbed some sparkle into her sleepy eyes, and we put on our heavy coats and boots.

The snow was wet and almost up to my knees as we waded toward the log barn. I carried a flashlight and Grandma carried a lantern. The sky was dark and the ground white. At the barn we wrestled with the heavy bar across the door. Grandma was wheezing. We got the door slightly open and I peeped in, Grandma right behind me. Juliet, MaryBelle and Oscar all had their own stalls and I didn't see a head in any of them like I could in the daytime. It was awfully quiet.

"Look," Grandma sounded excited, like a little girl. "They're bound to be kneeling. Not a head in sight, and you know horses sleep standing up."

"They're kneeling to the baby," I whispered. "It's right on the dot of midnight." Far away I heard a church bell or I thought I did.

"It's Christmas, all right," Grandma said. "Let's get back to the fire before we catch our deaths of cold."

In the light of the lantern, I could see a glow on Grandma's face. I wouldn't swear on a stack of bibles our animals had been kneeling, but I'd never tell Grandma that.

When we opened the door and kicked off our snowy boots, Mama was up. She'd made hot cocoa for us. The steaming cups smelled like Christmas.

She hugged me. "Look what Santa left for you...while you were out there in the cold."

She handed me a long box, all wrapped up in red and green paper. It looked just like a box a doll would come in. I didn't want any sissy doll with icy blue eyes. I was my daddy's tomboy. I was careful, hardly tearing the paper at all. I took the lid off.

It was a soldier boy doll. It had a khaki uniform on, even a cap with a stripe. His hair was as black as his painted boots. He was the handsomest soldier ever–just like my daddy. When I lifted him from the box and set him on the floor he was half as tall as I was. His buttons gleamed.

"He's all the way from Daddy's army camp," Mama said softly. "Your daddy sent him to you across the ocean all that way."

"My own soldier boy doll." It was a miracle. Like my daddy was with us. Santa had found us. The animals had knelt. It was Christmas.